Zio The Hero

To Sophie
Happy Reading

MARC GRIMSTON

Regards,
Marc Grimston

SECOND EDITION

2013

First Published 2011 by FASTPRINT PUBLISHING

Original artwork by Mike Allard

Cover design by Toby Breckels

ISBN: 1 4802 7543 3
ISBN-13: 978 148027 5430

To the real Rebekah,

Tobias, Nathaniel

and Adam,

With all my love,

Dad.

ZIO THE HERO

1

The sun streamed in through Robert's bedroom window, he yawned, reached over and switched off his alarm clock. If he had known that one of his brothers would be threatened with death, he would have pulled the bed covers back over his head and gone back to sleep. As he didn't, he got out of bed and put on the school clothes that he had left in a heap at the bottom of his bed. His father had told him to put them in the wash the night before but as usual he had forgotten, again. Once he was dressed he went to wake up his twin 8-year-old brothers Timothy and Michael who slept in the next room. Michael was awake in seconds and dressed almost as fast. Timothy on the other hand was always a pain to wake as he never went to sleep until he knew his Father was in bed.

Once the boys were dressed they went down for breakfast which they knew would be ready on the table as it always was. Their dad had always done the same thing every morning. He got up at 6am, had coffee before having a shower and getting the boys' cereal and toast ready for them when they came down at 7:15. The boys' mother had died when the twins were born and their father had given up a well-paid job working for the government and decided to dedicate his life to bringing up his sons.

This morning, however, was different, the kitchen was quiet and breakfast was not on the table.

"Dad!" called Timothy. "Where's my breakfast? I'm hungry." There was no reply. The house was still as the grave. Robert, who was just over two years older than the twins, took charge. "Right Michael, you go and look for dad in his room and in his study. Timothy, you look in our rooms and I'll check down here and we'll meet back in the kitchen."

Five minutes later the three boys were worried, very worried. Timothy was crying, Michael was wiping his nose and sniffing loudly and Robert was trying to be grown-up but was scared. The boys had never been left on their own before. Their father had given up weekends away with his friends; he told everyone that nothing in the world was more important than his boys. Robert always felt himself grow taller whenever his father said that. Today, however, they had checked the whole house but could not find him.

"There is one room we have not checked, the cellar," Michael sniffed. The other boys looked at him nervously.

"You know we aren't allowed down there. Last time I got caught coming up the cellar stairs I wasn't allowed out for a week."

"Well I don't care, I'm going to look and if I get told off I'll say I was scared."

Slowly the three boys opened the cellar door and peered down the stairs.

"Dad, are you there?"

"Don't be silly," said Robert, "the light is off."

Michael wiped his nose on the back of his hand again. Robert had made up his mind; he reached up, switched on the light and started down the stairs with Timothy and Michael close behind.

The cellar smelt musty and damp and cobwebs hung from the ceiling.

"I'm scared," whimpered Timothy.

Michael pointed to the corner, "What's that behind those boxes?"

The boys moved some old boxes and slowly an old wooden door became more apparent. The door was oak, had a big round handle and long black hinges, the sort of door you might find in a church.

Robert was the first to say what they were all thinking. "I have been down here lots of times but I've never seen that door before, have you?" Both boys shook their heads.

It was Timothy who made the first move. Slowly, very slowly, he reached out his hand, took hold of the old rusty handle and turned it. There was a clunk as the handle turned. The boys jumped.

"Come on you two give me a hand. I can't open it on my own."

Robert and Michael looked at each other, shrugged, and got hold of the door. Together they pulled it towards them. It took all their strength but bit by bit, and with a lot of creaking, the door opened.

As the door opened it revealed a long, dark, stone passage which was lit by flaming torches on both sides. Rats scurried away as the boys looked in. Large creepers hung down from the ceiling and water trickled down the walls and along the floor.

The boys looked at each other, they were all scared. Michael stepped inside.

"Come on, let's find dad. I want my breakfast."

"I don't like rats," said Robert.

"Neither do I but we must find dad he might be in danger. Come on let's go!"

The boys pushed their way down the passage. It seemed to go on forever and as they went further along it started to get cold. Timothy shivered.

"I don't like this. Please, can we go back?"

Michael looked at his twin and shook his head.

"We must find dad. Come on, he can't be far now."

Slowly the passage started to widen and became clearer. In the distance a small door came into view. Cautiously the boys approached it. The door only came up to Robert's shoulders; the handle on this door gleamed proudly.

Robert was the first to smell it.

"I can smell food and it smells like daddy's cooking!"

"Wait!" said Timothy, as he grabbed at Robert who had been about to open the door. "It might be a trap."

Robert gasped and swallowed hard. "I hadn't thought of that, sorry."

Both boys looked at Timothy. He had turned very pale.

"Whatever's the matter?"

"L…l…look," stammered Timothy, pointing behind his brothers, who were facing away from the door. Both boys turned, then Michael turned pale and Robert backed away. Whilst they had been talking the door had been opened, from the OTHER SIDE, and in the doorway stood a very large man. Well, they thought it was a large man. They could only see the bottom half of him because the door was so small.

A big, dirty and smelly hand reached through the door, grabbed Michael and pulled him through. Timothy tried to scream but it only came out as a squeak. One after the other the boys were pulled through. They found that they had come through a door set into the back of a fireplace. The boys looked out into the room in front of them. It was a large room with stone walls and they could see a straw roof above them. The room smelt of wood smoke, pots and pans hung from the walls, the furniture was made from roughly cut wood and the window was just a hole in the wall.

"Hello," boomed a deep, gruff voice.

The boys spun around and took in the rest of the man they had seen in the doorway. He was large and heavy and his belly hung below his coarsely woven shirt.

"My name is Tregore," said the man.

The boys all noticed at the same time that Tregore was holding something in his hand; an axe, a very large one. Robert felt his head start to spin. He looked at his brothers and noticed that they had gone pale as well. Michael looked at the axe and he felt his feet go from under him. The boys all passed out.

2

When the boys came round they were all sitting in high backed, wooden chairs in front of the fire which had now been lit. Tregore was busying himself round a large cooking pot. The boys looked at each other, each hoping they were not going to be put into the pot. Robert took a sideways look at the axe which was now stuck into one of the logs by the fire and gulped. Tregore must have heard the gulp for he turned round with a big soup ladle in his hand. The boys tried to shrink into their chairs. Tregore looked at the boys and noticed Robert staring at the axe. He laughed so loudly that his belly wobbled. "Do you think..." he was laughing so much that he had to sit down. "Do you think I'm going to chop you up and cook you for me supper?" he said, smiling.

"Well," began Robert, "we saw the axe and your big cooking pot and, well we, er..."

"Never mind about the axe that's just me job. You boys must be hungry after such a long time, it's long past breakfast time. You will need some food in your bellies before you meet the King."

While he was speaking, Tregore had taken three wooden plates from the shelf above the fire and put a ladle of 'goo' onto each. He handed the plates to the boys. "Eat up," he said, in a rising voice.

"Er, I don't want to be rude," Robert began, "but please, what is it?"

"Why lad that's the King's best venison. You are very honored to eat such fine fare. No ordinary folk gets to eat it."

Robert picked at the food before him but Timothy who ate anything was soon wiping his mouth with the back of his hand and asking for more. Tregore smiled and put another ladle of stew on Timothy's plate.

Michael coughed to get Tregore's attention, and asked nervously, "About the axe, what's your job then?"

"Me job?" Tregore walked over to the axe and pulled it from the log. He held it like a mother would hold her baby, lovingly. "Me job? Why, I'm the King's executioner, I chops people's heads off. It's a bit messy at times, but not too bad, if I remember to sharpen me axe."

Robert, who had managed to eat only a bit of the stew, was nearly sick. Michael managed a feeble, "Oh," before he ran to the door and was sick outside. Timothy carried on eating.

"Now don't you boys worry, I only chops heads off the King's enemies and seeing as you three were expected I reckon you be friends."

"What do you mean, 'expected'," began Robert, "and who is the King anyway?"

"Never mind 'bout that for now, there'll be plenty of time for all that later. You'll need to eat up 'n' rest before you sees the King on the morrow."

"On the morrow?" Timothy looked confused. "I think he means tomorrow morning, I remember doing Old English in history at school," Robert said.

"Tomorrow morning," moaned Timothy. "What about our dad? We still haven't found him yet; he will be worried."

Tregore smiled quietly to himself, but said nothing. Slowly the boys began to feel tired, and their heads began to nod. One by one the boys dropped their bowls; the remainder of their stew spilled out across the cold stone floor. Tregore moved quickly and caught the boys, as one by one they fell from their chairs, and he put them onto his big bed. Robert had been the last to fall asleep. Tregore had expected this. After all, Robert had only a small amount of the stew with the sleeping potion in it. After Tregore had put Robert onto the bed and covered all the boys with animal skins to keep them warm he settled down in his chair by the fire; it was going to be a long night. He picked up his axe and slowly he sharpened it lovingly, a smile slowly spreading across his face.

****

Robert woke with a start wondering why his alarm had not gone off. He turned to look at the clock to see what the time was but found himself looking into the face of his brother Michael who had also just woken, also thinking he was at home in his own bed. Then both boys looked at Timothy who was still fast asleep, probably dreaming about playing with his toys. Robert reached over and shook Timothy until he woke with a start. "What, what time…"

"Shh." Michael put his hand over Timothy's mouth and pointed to Tregore who was muttering to himself while stirring the huge cooking pot which was hanging over the fire. Timothy's eyes opened wide as he realized where he was and that he was still a long way from home.

Tregore had not heard the boys awaken, or at least if he had he pretended he hadn't. He just continued to stir the pot.

The boys looked at each other and very quietly got out of the bed and began to creep towards the door. As Robert opened it the door gave a loud creak. Tregore turned and froze them in his stare.

"Mornin' boys," he said, "glad to see you slept well. The stream is out back if you want to wash."

The boys looked at each other and went out to find the stream. While they washed, they plotted. Tregore seemed like a nice man but Robert couldn't be sure.

"How are we going to get away and find our way home?" Robert asked in desperation, more to himself than the others. For what seemed like ages the boys sat by the stream, trying to work out a way to escape. Michael pointed out that ever since they had arrived the fire had been lit, so they wouldn't be able to get back through the little door behind the fireplace. That way was out.

They did not hear Tregore approaching as they talked.

"Well," he said, "all nice 'n' clean to see the King. Come and have your breakfast, you've got a busy day ahead of you."

Slowly the boys got up and went back with Tregore,

cross with themselves that they had not made a run for it while they could have.

As they all went in, the bushes behind the stream moved and a girl of about twelve stood up and stretched. She had been listening in on the boy's conversation but no one had seen her. Rebekah was confused; she did not understand why they had been talking about Tregore's fireplace. Her head spun with questions. She took a drink from the stream and headed back to the castle.

Tobias who had been sent down by the King to keep an eye on Princess Rebekah got up slowly from his hiding place too but he did not go back the castle. Instead, he sat down by the stream and waited. He thought that he was going to have to wait a long time but he was wrong, very wrong.

3

As the boys entered the cottage Tregore got them to sit down and handed each one of them a wooden bowl and a spoon. He went back to the cooking pot and brought it over to them, dipped a ladle into it and lifted out some slop, splattering spoonfuls into each bowl.

"What is…" began Robert.

"Porridge, eat up. It's all there is, and it will fill you up."

"I like porridge," said Timothy, stuffing his face.

"Can I have a drink please, I'm thirsty?" asked Michael.

"Jug's over by the fire, stream is outside," said Tregore, without thinking.

Michael jumped up, grabbed the jug and headed for the door. Tregore realized what was happening.

"Stop!" he shouted, but he was too late. Michael had gone, only to return seconds later with Tobias close behind.

Tobias turned angrily to Tregore.

"Tregore! I was told that you would use the cart to take our guests to the castle. What has happened to the plan?"

Tregore muttered his apology, "Sorry, I didn't think about the children needing something to drink."

Tobias muttered something to himself that no one heard and walked over to the fireplace and stared into the flames, trying to work out what to do next. The plan had been to get the boys to eat drugged bread with their breakfast and whilst they were asleep to take them to the castle in the cart so when they had woken up they would have been safely locked away in the dungeon. Tobias kicked the plate of drugged bread into the fire as it was no longer needed. None of the boys noticed. Robert made the first move; he went up to Tobias who he guessed was about his own age, reached out his hand and said, "Hello, my name is Robert, what's yours?"

"Tobias."

Timothy looked at his twin, "What a funny name."

"And funny clothes," said Michael. Both the twins started to giggle.

Robert looked at Tregore.

"What is this about a cart and a castle?"

"Ah! Well, it is like this," began Tregore. "Young Tobias 'ere was sent down by the King to escort you to the castle. It's a long way, so we thought the cart would be quicker." (Tregore failed to mention the sleeping potion or the dungeon.)

"I don't want to go to see the King or his castle, I want my dad, he will be worried," moaned Michael, wiping his nose on his school sweatshirt.

"I DON'T CARE ABOUT YOUR FATHER BUT YOU ARE GOING TO SEE THE KING! EVEN IF YOU HAZ TO BE DRAGGED THERE BEHIND THE CART!" shouted Tregore.

Tregore stood in the doorway, reached down and picked up a coil of rope. The boys became scared and fell quiet.

Tobias stepped in between Tregore and the frightened boys his mind made up. He might have been only 11 but he was there in the name of the King.

"Tregore," Tobias demanded, "what do you think you are doing, have you forgotten who these boys are? Don't you forget they are under the King's protection."

Tregore's face reddened with guilt and he put down the rope.

"I'm sorry boys," he began, "I weren't thinking. You are the King's guests and it weren't right o' me to scare you all like I has done." He held out his hand to Robert.

Robert remained still and didn't move towards the big, ugly man. Robert had decided Tregore was the sort of bad man his father had warned him about.

"We still want to know where our dad is," said Robert.

Tregore and Tobias looked at each other.

"Well, we might as well tell them," said Tobias. Tregore sat down and motioned for the boys to do the same.

"This is going to be difficult for you to understand," Tobias said. "About five years ago an ancient scroll was found in an underground cavern under the King's castle near the sea. The prophecy said that the crown of England would be lost and three boys in strange clothes would come to search for it. Two months ago the King's crown went missing and the whole kingdom has been waiting for you to come, and now you are here."

"But where is here?" began Robert. "And we don't have a King we have a Queen."

Tobias looked at Robert and said, "We do have a Queen,

King Christian's wife! Queen Gwendolyn."

"Don't talk rubbish."

Robert felt his hand clenching into a fist. He hated fighting; his father had always told him that it wouldn't get him anywhere. He also hated looking stupid. He was considering thumping Tobias when Tregore pushed in between them. Looking at Robert he shook his head.

"Tobias is of the King's household and if any 'arm is done to him the punishment is death. Do you want me to 'ave to use the axe?"

Looking at the ground Robert suddenly felt hot and he could feel his face turning red.

"No," he muttered, with a lump in his throat.

Timothy moved to stand beside his brother. "If you try, you will have to take me on as well," he said.

"STOP!" Tobias shouted, raising his arm. "Enough of this silliness; the boys are expected. Let us remember that they are protected by royal command."

All this time Michael had been looking out the window, thinking. He turned and sat down, the light from the sun shining across his face. "If you say there is a King, and we know that there is not, maybe we are all right."

Tobias looked at him. "What do you mean?"

Michael walked over to the others and sat down.

"Well, I know that where I live we have a Queen, but I don't live here. So where are we?"

Tregore and Tobias looked at each other and shrugged their shoulders. "Tunstall Woods in England, of course," said Tregore.

"Sorry, I mean when are we?"

"What do you mean?"

"Well," began Michael, "I mean what year is it?"

Tobias smiled to himself but managed to look surprised.

"Everyone knows that."

Robert and Timothy had gone very quiet, as if they almost knew the answer.

"It is the fifth year of King Christian's reign, 1384."

Timothy and Robert looked at each other.

"But it can't be," began Timothy.

Michael walked over to his brothers and looked at them.

"But it is, and we are here."

Confused, Robert and Timothy looked at each other as they sat in shock then looked at their brother. Suddenly they knew the impossible had happened. Somehow they had done what they had only read about in stories. They did not know how or why but they knew that they had traveled back in time. And if they had known what lay ahead of them, they would have gone back through the door in the fireplace, fire or no fire.

4

Rebekah sang to herself as she skipped back up to the castle. She didn't understand what all the fuss was about. The boys she had been spying on seemed unsure where they were, and they had such funny clothes on. They had been dressed in their school uniforms and she had giggled as she remembered looking at them.

As she approached the castle she became aware that one of the guards was running out to meet her.

"Princess Rebekah, your father is very cross with you. You know you are not allowed to leave the castle without an escort."

"Father knows that I like going into the forest. Anyway I know he sent Tobias to watch over me; he is not very good at hiding."

Rebekah remembered that when she had been watching Tregore's hut she had seen Tobias' reflection in the stream.

"Run and tell my father that the guests he has been waiting for will be here soon."

The guard stopped and was about to say something but thought better of it and bowed instead.

"At once Princess," and with that he was gone. "And stop calling me Princess," she shouted after him, "everybody knows I hate being called that."

"Sorry Princess," the guard called back over his shoulder, as he disappeared in through a pair of big oak doors of the castle.

****

Tobias was getting cross; things had not gone to plan. By now the boys should have been locked in the dungeon, waiting to be summoned by the King to look for the crown. Instead, they were sitting by the stream, as if Tobias and the boys had all been friends for years. Tobias did not trust these boys with their strange ways and clothes. He decided to take charge.

"Right!" he said, as he stood up. "We must go to the castle and see the King now. We have spent too long chatting. It is a long walk and we are late already."

"Late for what?" asked Timothy

"Dinner."

Timothy jumped up.

"Let's go then, I was just thinking how hungry I am."

"You're always hungry. I still think we should be looking for dad though," muttered Robert, as he got to his feet.

Tregore got up and taking hold of Michael's hand pulled him onto his feet.

"Let's get goin' then."

Tregore was trying to look as if he were in charge but he knew that he was going to have to go along with whatever Tobias said.

Turning to Tobias, Tregore said "I'll get the cart then.".

"No, we'll walk, we don't need the cart now do we?"

Tregore remembered the rope and old clothes in the cart

and realised that they no longer needed to tie the boys up and force them to the castle.

"Ahh, 'tis a nice day for a walk."

Slowly, the group started to walk through the forest. Timothy kept asking over and over what they were going to have for dinner. Robert was thinking his own thoughts. He still didn't like Tregore. Why had he brought his axe along with him, he wondered?

Michael wandered along, looking up at the trees, wishing he had one like these in his garden to climb. He suddenly remembered his father had promised to get a climbing frame for him and his brothers. He wondered if he would ever see him again. He bit his lip, hoping that no one had seen his shoulders fall as he let out a sigh. The trees were difficult to see now as he fought back the tears.

"Are we nearly there yet?"

"Not long now," Tobias and Tregore answered together.

****

The throne room was strangely quiet. Normally there were lots of people trying to ask the King for advice. Usually people would be lining up waiting their turn. But not today. Today the King sat sideways on his throne, his feet over one of the arms. Good thing the Queen couldn't see him, he thought to himself. Rebekah and her two brothers Nathaniel and Adam were playing quietly at the end of the room. A few royal servants were rushing about trying to look as if they had plenty to do. A guard stood each side of the throne. Two others stood by the door. No one had come to ask for advice for some time. After all, no one knew what to say to a King with no crown.

Suddenly, the door at the far end of the throne room flew open and in stormed Baron Blackheart. The guards moved towards him to stop him but he ushered them away with a slight wave of his hand.

"Your Majesty, how are you? It has been such a long time since anyone came to seek your advice. How long has it been now? Two months? Such a shame you've only got one month left to find the crown, haven't you? I do so hope those children are found and they find it for you. It would be such a shame if you have to hand over the throne to your daughter."

King Christian pointed his finger at Blackheart.

"I am well aware of the law stating if the crown of England is lost for three months, the King or Queen must hand over the country to the oldest child."

Rebekah ran to her father and threw her arms round him.

"Oh Father I don't want to be Queen. I'm not old enough."

The King comforted his daughter, stroking her hair.

"I'm sure that the boys will come and…"

"But Father," Rebekah interrupted, "the boys are here. I saw them at Tregore's hut in the forest and they have strange clothes just like the prophecy foretold. Tregore and Tobias are bringing them here now."

The King leapt out of his throne, as if he'd been stung.

"Gwendolyn, where are you my dear? Guard, go at once and fetch the Queen."

The guard nearly jumped out of his skin. In his rush to do the King's bidding he dropped his spear as he ran from the room.

Blackheart was in shock, he had been told that as soon as the children were seen they would be killed so the throne could become his. But he quickly recovered himself hoping that no one had seen his surprise.

"But Your Majesty, they are only children. How can they help the great King of England?" sneered Blackheart. "Now, as your friend and advisor I urge you to step down and let Rebekah become Queen. I will be her advisor and I will help her until she is old enough to rule on her own."

The King turned on Baron Blackheart.

"SILENCE! DO YOU TAKE ME FOR A FOOL?" bellowed the King. "I know that you only want the throne for yourself. You have no interest in helping my daughter or the royal family; all you want to do is look after own interests. GET OUT! You are banished and no longer a royal advisor!"

The Baron turned on his heel and stormed out of the room. He shouted as he left, "Making an enemy of me will be your undoing. I will do everything in my power to stop those boys finding your crown. They will be dead before the month is out."

Outside the castle a trumpet sounded announcing the arrival of Tobias, Tregore and three small boys in strange clothes. The boys did not realise the whole country was looking to them and hoping they would be heroes as foretold.

5

"Sire," a guard ran into the room, stopped, bowed low and continued, "sire, the foretold ones are coming."

"You idiot! Do you think I am stupid? I know that. Now get out of my way. I will await their arrival in the dungeon."

"But sire, they are not sleeping. I know that Tregore was meant to drug them and bring them in the cart, but…" The guard looked at the floor and muttered the rest of what he wanted to say, "…sire, they are very much awake."

"What do you mean, awake?"

"I mean they are walking sire, with Tobias and Tregore."

The guard again averted his eyes from the King, he knew that when the King gave an order it was to be carried out to the letter and the children should have been tied and gagged in the cart. The soldier waited for the King to scream at him.

The King pushed the guard to one side as he walked towards a window to see outside. The guard staggered but managed to keep on his feet. Below the castle the King could see Tregore, Tobias and the boys walking up the path towards the castle gate. The Queen joined her husband at the window while he watched. Queen Gwendolyn did not look like most queens. She was short, plump and had a face the size of a dinner plate.

"Well darling, these children might help us without you threatening them. Try asking for help occasionally, rather than demanding it all the time," she said quietly. The King said nothing but he muttered something under his breath.

The two princes were pushing and shoving each other at a different window, trying to get a better look at these strange children.

Nathaniel was nine years old and for his age, one of the best archers in the land. Adam at seven thought he was a great archer too but he often got distracted when he was aiming and as a result usually ended up shooting in the wrong direction, hitting anything but the target.

Below, as the party approached, the three boys looked around; they were all stunned by the size of the castle and its majesty. Michael got the feeling that he had been to the castle before but he realised he had never been to a castle quite like this. All the castles he had seen had been in ruins not brand new like this one. The castle was huge. It had towers at each corner and two more in the middle from which a drawbridge was being lowered with a low rumble. Flags flew from the tops of all the towers.

As the party neared the castle the sun dazzled them as it reflected off the armour of the knights who stood along the battlements. With the clatter of hooves, two knights on horseback came trotting from the castle towards them. Behind the mounted knights came twenty more as a show of power, all marching briskly, ten behind each horse.

Timothy looked at Tobias, "What do we do now?"

Tobias strode forward; the knights each side of him

stood smartly and did not move. Tobias spoke quietly to one of the knights who stepped aside and let the boy pass. Timothy noticed some of them had their swords drawn and he thought that blood was dripping off one of them but in the bright sunlight it was difficult to be sure. Robert noticed a knight in black armour with a red plume flowing out from his helmet galloping away from the rear of the castle. If he had known the rider was Blackheart he would have turned pale. Baron Blackheart was off to find other barons and lords who owed him favours.

As Tobias left the others the knights closed in on the boys and Tregore, enclosing them in a ring of armour. The boys huddled together and Tregore approached one of the knights. The knight shook his head and drew his sword just a little. Tregore backed off. Two of the knights stepped to one side and Tobias, accompanied by a man in a bright purple cape, strode into the circle. Michael and his brothers all noticed he was wearing a black shiny breastplate and on it, in red, was a lion's head. Its mouth was open as if it were roaring. "My name is Sir Kempston Baignard. Come with me. The King is waiting."

As he turned, Robert noticed the same lion on Sir Baignard's cape. He nudged Michael.

"I think he must be important."

The knights formed a tight group round the boys as they made their way into the castle. Michael and Robert noticed carvings of roaring lions all around them but Timothy noticed the smell of cooking.

"Food!" he exclaimed and realised he was still hungry.

The throne room which had been quiet shortly before was now full of people, all trying to get a glimpse of the three small boys who were there to save the King. As the party neared the King a guard stood in the way.

"Only the King's personal bodyguards are allowed to carry weapons in the presence of the King," he said stiffly.

Tregore blushed, muttered an apology and handed the guard his axe, who leaned it against the wall.

As the boys looked round, they could see that the room was huge. Robert thought his whole house would fit into just this one room! It was decorated with gold and purple banners all with the same roaring lion on them. Tables had been put along the edges of the room and the throne, made of beautiful carved oak, stood imposingly at the far end.

On the arms of the throne were sitting lions, with their mouths open, as if roaring. The King was tall. Michael thought very tall. He was wearing the most fantastic blue and purple cloak over very expensive clothes and boots that came up to his knees. Robert thought he looked better than the pictures of kings he had seen in school books. He had a short grey beard and Robert could see a few grey hairs on an otherwise bald head. He was also obviously a lot older than the Queen. She was sitting on a smaller throne to the right of her husband and the children were sitting to the left of their father. Rebekah and Nathaniel were seated but Adam was standing on his seat leaning over the back and was watching a beetle as it scurried across the floor. The King reached over and tapped him. Adam sat down.

As the boys approached the throne, they could hear people talking about them.

"Look at their funny clothes."

"Aren't they small?"

"How can they help us? They are too skinny."

The boys felt themselves becoming more and more self-conscious.

The King rose to his feet.

The room fell silent.

CRASH!!!

Everyone turned to see what had made the noise. Tregore's axe lay on the floor.

"TREGORE!!" roared the King. "Why have you brought your axe into the throne room?"

"Er, I am sorry sire but I was not thinking. The axe goes where I go."

"Not in my castle. Out with it!"

A guard picked up the axe and hurried out of the throne room. Michael and Timothy looked at each other and giggled.

"SILENCE!"

The boys stopped giggling.

The King turned his attention to the boys.

"So, you are the three boys who are to find the crown. You don't look very strong to me. How do you think you are going to manage?"

Robert, being the oldest, approached the King.

"Look here," he began, "we don't know anything about a crown; we just got up this morning and…"

"Yesterday morning," interrupted Timothy.

"…yesterday morning," corrected Robert, "got ready for school like we always do, went downstairs for breakfast and couldn't find our father so we looked round the house and ended up in the cellar. There was a door that we hadn't seen before and it led us to Tregore's house. All we want to do is find our dad and go home. We will be in a lot of trouble as it is for missing a day at school."

Michael sniffed loudly and wiped his nose on the cuff of his sweatshirt.

Timothy rubbed his tummy, he was still hungry. The King was beginning to get angry.

"I have heard enough about how you got here. There is a prophecy which foretells of your arrival and now you are here. So the question is are you going to help us to find the crown or are you going to be executed?"

Timothy spoke up for his brothers.

"We will help, but not until we have had something to eat!"

A ripple of laughter went through the assembled crowd.

6

The Queen stood up (not that anyone noticed, because she was so short).

"The young man is quite right, how can we ask him and his brothers to help us on an empty stomach? Guard, go and tell the cooks to prepare a feast, they have one hour." The Queen turned to her children. "These children are to be your guests, you are to show them round the castle and make them feel at home. Take Tobias with you. Now go."

"Yes Mother," Rebekah, Nathaniel and Adam said together.

The King looked uncomfortable; he hated it when Gwendolyn seemed to know what to do, and he didn't.

"Tregore," he said, trying to look as if he was in charge, "you will stay at the castle in case you are needed."

"Yes sire," replied Tregore, giving a low bow. He looked at Robert wondering how many blows it would take from his axe to chop off the child's head, if he failed to help the King. Two, maybe three, he decided, unless he remembered to sharpen the axe.

Robert shivered but was not sure why.

Rebekah took charge.

"Come on, we haven't got long before we eat and we have a lot to show you."

Timothy licked his lips; the thought of food was getting too much for him. Right now he would settle for a plate of peas, and he hated peas. Tobias went up to Robert.

"Look, I am sorry about all the fuss at Tregore's cottage. I didn't know you very well then, can we be friends? I'm all alone here at the castle and although the King and Queen are kind to me, there is no one my age and I think we both need a friend."

Robert held out his hand.

"Thank you," he whispered, a small lump rising in his throat, "I need a friend too. Will you help me to understand what is going on because I am not used to time travel yet."

Tobias smiled to himself, but only said, "I'll try," as he shook Robert's hand.

The two boys walked off chatting, not noticing that the rest of the group had not followed them.

****

"Princess Rebekah," a guard came running, "your father needs you in the royal chambers, right away."

"That means he wants me around so mother doesn't make him look silly in front of all those people. Not that he needs help to look silly, he can do that all by himself," she added, as she followed the guard.

Timothy and Michael were left with Nathaniel and Adam.

"I am Timothy and this is Michael, we are twins."

"Oh sorry, I am rude, I am Nathaniel and this is Adam my brother. My sister is called Rebekah, and she is very bossy."

"Are you really princes?" asked Michael.

"Yes, I am sorry to say."

Timothy and Michael looked at each other; they had never seen a real prince before and didn't know what to say. It was Timothy who asked what they were both thinking.

"Do we have to call you sir or something?"

"Oh no, please don't, we couldn't stand it. We are princes because our parents are the King and Queen but I wish we were ordinary peasants, like you."

Timothy and Michael had never had been called peasants before, they were not sure how to take it.

7

Baron Blackheart had been busy, very busy. He was sitting in his castle in a small room at the top of the tallest tower rubbing his hands together and laughing to himself. The King had only a short time left, and then he would become Rebekah's guardian and be in charge of the country. The princess would either become his wife when she was older, or she would die.

Blackheart thought death was a better idea, but he had to come up with an accident, maybe she could fall from her horse and be trampled. Horses can make a mess of a child, such a shame. He smiled and laughed to himself as he thought of more and more horrid ways to kill the princess. Suddenly the door to his room flew open and crashed against the wall. The Baron jumped.

"So sorry to disturb you Master," a voice muttered.

The Baron turned, and there in the doorway stood a small hunched-up figure dressed in old tatty clothes that long ago had been smart. The smell coming from the man told Blackheart that the clothes had not been washed for ages. He had dirty fingernails, unkempt dirty black hair and strangely piercing blue eyes that stared out of a small, unwashed face.

"Duncan, what do you mean by coming in here when

I'm thinking? Can't you see that I'm busy?" shouted the Baron as he opened a window to get rid of the smell that had entered the room the same time as the servant.

"I'm sorry to disturb you sire but the people you summoned have all now arrived."

"Good, go and tell the cook to prepare food for 20 guests. We shall be served in the Great Hall."

"At once master."

Blackheart smiled to himself. "At last!" he said, even though there was no one to hear him. He had sent for other barons and lords who were unhappy with the way that King Christian was ruling. Together they would come up with a plan to get rid of the three small boys who were threatening Blackheart's path to the throne. Slowly Blackheart started down the stairs stroking his beard as he plotted.

The Great Hall was a large hall but could hardly be called great. A long, roughly-cut wooden table stood in the middle of the room, and to one side of the room there was a crumbling fireplace, which had not seen a fire in a very long time. Hanging around the room were the remains of banners and flags that were so faded that it was hard to see what colour they had once been. The guests were at one end of the room. They were talking in low whispers and they kept looking over their shoulders to make sure no one else was listening.

"Gentlemen."

The men turned and there, in the middle of the room, stood Baron Blackheart.

"Come and sit down. Food will soon be here and we have much to discuss."

As he spoke the door at the far end of the room opened and in walked the cook with two scruffy servants, who carried trays of bread and cheese and a cask of ale. The barons and lords came over to the table and sitting on long benches started to eat. Duncan walked around the table and from a large bag he carried with him, he put a smaller leather bag in front of each guest. As he did so, each bag was shaken and tucked out of sight beneath their cloaks. The money could be heard to jingle as each bag was shaken.

Blackheart again smiled to himself; how easy it was to get people to do what he wanted. All it took was some food and a small bag of gold.

A tall, good-looking knight was the first to address their host.

"So Blackheart, what have you called us here for? We have enough trouble keeping our own lands and villages without helping you to keep yours."

There were nods and grunts from all round the table.

"As you all know the King has er, lost his crown."

Some of those round the table started to laugh. Blackheart held up his hand, the room fell silent.

"And you all know that unless the crown is found the King has only got one month left before he loses the throne. It is our duty to make sure the crown is never found. The three boys that were mentioned in the prophecy are here, we must kill them before they get near the hiding place."

There were more nods and grunts of approval from around the room.

The tall, good-looking knight (who was called Lord Hampstead) said what they were all thinking.

"What we need now is some ideas of ways to dispose of those wretched boys."

Blackheart agreed.

"But it must look like an accident. If we were simply to put an arrow through each of their chests it would be a lot quicker for us, but we would have the King's guards rushing around."

"But why would that matter?" asked Lord Hampstead

"Because they might stumble across the crown's hiding place and then our plans would come to nothing."

All the barons and lords nodded, and started to talk about how they could kill the boys.

While they had been talking, no one had noticed a man enter the room and stand in the shadows. He had listened to the plotting and scheming but said nothing. As the guests started to leave, the man in the shadows slowly and silently left the room, glad that he had not been seen.

8

Nathaniel turned to Michael. "Would you like to see my pet dragon?"

"Pardon?" said Michael and Timothy together. "Did you say a pet dragon?"

"Of course, haven't you got a pet?"

"Well, yes we have. We have a pet hamster we keep in the shed, and he's called Ginger."

"Oh," said Adam, "we eat hamsters."

"Not Ginger you don't," said Timothy.

Nathaniel grabbed hold of Michael's arm. "Come on," he said, "we have lots to show you."

****

"Wow! That is the biggest climbing frame I have ever seen!" exclaimed Robert, as he and Tobias came round the corner into the courtyard. He broke into a run and before Tobias could stop him he had started to climb. Robert was a very good climber; at school he could climb the big tree in the playground before anyone else could, even before the bigger boys. Robert climbed hand over hand up towards the top. It was not as easy as it had first looked. Bits of the climbing frame moved as he got to them. Tobias, below, had gone very pale.

"Get down," he called up, as softly as he could, "before

you are seen."

"Come on up," shouted Robert, "don't be a sissy. I can see the sea from here."

A guard had seen them from the other side of the courtyard and he came running, drawing his sword as he ran and he called for help. Archers came running and aimed their bows at the climbing boy.

"Get down now or we will shoot." one of them called.

Robert nodded. "All right, don't shoot. I'll come down."

Robert started to climb down thinking the guard was a spoilsport. Tobias grabbed his new friend by the arm and together they ran into the castle.

****

Adam grabbed hold of Timothy's arm and started to pull him along.

"Come on this is the way to the Stables, our Dragon lives there".

Michael looked at his twin and started to follow Adam. Before they got very far there was a deep booming sound coming from deep within the castle walls. The two boys looked at each other,

"Come on, we had better go," said Nathaniel.

"What was that?" both the visitors said together.

"That is the call to the feast."

"FEAST! At last."

Timothy started to trot back towards the castle.

The four boys arrived back in the Great Hall at a run, Timothy in front. As they entered, Tobias and Robert came in at the other end of the room. Both boys were giggling.

"Shh," giggled Tobias. "It was a good thing that the guard was a friend of mine, or you would have been in real trouble."

"How was I to know what it was? I've never seen a trebuchet before."

"But I told you not to climb it; it's a sort of catapult."

Both boys were giggling and trying not to be seen.

Michael noticed them and was glad that they now seemed to have become friends; he remembered the fight that had nearly taken place in Tregore's cottage.

A long table had been put down the middle of the room, servants stood at both ends and down the sides. At the far end of the room stood another table that had a large seat in the middle and to the right was a smaller one. All the rest of the seating was less imposing. Round the room stood all the guests, all of whom had stopped to stare as the children came running in. Timothy was the first to see all the food laid out along the middle of the table. He rushed over to the nearest seat, sat down and started to reach for a chicken leg. He felt a sharp pain across the back of his hand as Sir Kempston Baignard rapped it.

"Oww!"

"We do not sit until the King has sat, and we do not eat until we are told that we can."

"Worse than school," muttered Timothy, but he got up all the same.

A trumpet blast sounded and a door at the far end of the room opened. All the people bowed low, and in walked the King, Queen and Princess Rebekah. Nathaniel and Adam left the other children and went and stood quietly with their parents. The King was the first to sit followed by the Queen to his right and Rebekah to the left and the boys sat to the right of their mother. The room fell silent. The King reached out and picked up a chicken leg, this was the sign for all the people to sit and eat. Timothy dived at the food excitedly.

After the meal, a knight stepped forward with a large scroll. He cleared his throat, unrolled the scroll and began to read.

"It is with great pleasure that the King welcomes Robert, Timothy and Michael to the castle. These children are to fulfil the ancient prophecy and find the lost crown. The King has decreed that all help will be given to the children and they will be given authority to go wherever they choose. Anyone found to be hindering them will be beheaded."

The King stood and the room fell silent.

Sir Kempston Baignard went over to where the three guests from the future sat. Quietly he knelt down by Robert's chair and spoke to the boy.

"You and your brothers must now approach the King."

Robert scraped his chair across the floor as he stood. Timothy and Michael also got up and together they walked up to the King. As they walked the rest of the guests one by one stood as three small boys walked past. The King met the children and put his arm on Robert's shoulder.

"These children are now under my protection, anything that they ask for will be granted to them. Anyone helping them will be rewarded, and as I have decreed, anyone hindering them in their work will be executed."

The boys returned to their seats, none of them realising the importance of the ceremony that had just taken place. As they walked down the hall all the other guests bowed to them.

****

While the King and his guests had been eating, a door had been opened at the back of the castle. No one had noticed that a man in black armour with a red plume on his helmet had crept in.

9

Blackheart knew the castle like the back of his hand; he knew while the King and the children were eating he could find out what the King was planning. He found an empty storeroom and with the help of a spy inside the castle he changed out of his armour into dark clothing. The Baron then made his way slowly towards the main hall. As he rounded the last corner Blackheart stopped in time to see a guard standing in front of the large oak doors. He cursed his bad luck and shrunk into the shadows. Normally, King Christian was not bothered with security, because he felt that as everybody loved him he had nothing to fear. The Baron laughed to himself as he thought of how stupid the King was. The guard must have heard the laugh as he turned towards the noise. Blackheart put his hand over his mouth and shrunk back further against the wall. The guard was not happy with what he had heard and drawing his sword he approached Blackheart. Blackheart quietly drew his dagger, he knew that a dead guard would cause awkward questions, but if he was caught that would be the end of his plans.

Then the door of the hall opened and the boys came running out closely followed by Rebekah who was trying to keep control of her brothers but failing. The guard turned and went back to his post by the great oak doors, never knowing that he had been only seconds from death.

"Come on," said Nathaniel, "you haven't seen our pet Zio yet, he lives in one of the stables."

Timothy looked at the prince. "Zio?"

"Zio is our dragon"

Michael giggled. "Zio, what a silly name!"

"In dragon language Zio means brave and fearless one. We called him that because he is not brave or fearless!"

"Your Highnesses," a guard had followed them from the hall, "Her Majesty the Queen has ordered me to tell you that you are due to go to your bed chamber soon and she will have one of the servants check that you are there!"

"Oh, that means we will have to be quick!"

The children ran on down the passage. Blackheart held his breath; he had heard every word that had been said. Had he wanted to he had been close enough to reach out and grab Robert who had been only inches from his hiding place. After they had gone the Baron melted away, thankful his dark clothes had hidden him so well. As he went he smiled, a plan slowly forming in his evil mind.

****

"Oh wow!" the three boys exclaimed together. They were standing in the doorway of what had once been a block of three stables that had now been knocked in to one large room. There in the middle of the straw-strewn room stood a large bright yellow dragon. The boys were unable to speak. Timothy had brought a chicken leg with him from the hall as a snack for later, and he dropped it in awe.

"I thought dragons only existed in story books and I never thought they would be yellow!" Robert managed to say, "And now we've met a real one!"

Zio looked over to Robert.

"Ahhhchoo! Sorry, I have a terrible cold. Lots of people are surprised when they meet a dragon for the first time."

As the dragon sneezed a small ball of flame shot out of his nose and set fire to the straw at his feet. Zio stamped it out with one of his big feet.

"I'm yellow today because I'm happy but I can change to any colour that you like if that's better."

As he spoke Zio slowly turned green.

"I think this is a better colour as I don't feel very well."

Robert, Timothy and Michael all sat down suddenly on the straw behind them. Rebekah looked at her brothers and Tobias and shrugged her shoulders.

"Haven't you seen a dragon before? They are quiet common."

Zio turned to the princess.

"Don't call me common, I am a special sort of dragon I'll have you know. Not one of your common ones."

"Yes I know, because you were born in the castle you think you are royal don't you."

"Well, you were born in the castle and you are royal, so if you are, I must be too."

Nathaniel took Michael and Timothy to one side and whispered to them.

"Zio is a bit simple, but he is very loyal and that's what matters."

Robert looked at his brothers and was the first to speak.

"I guess that we had hoped that dragons might really exist, but we never imagined that they spoke!"

"Well how do you think we communicate with you mere humans then?" asked Zio.

Before any of the boys could answer a servant came running.

"Your Highnesses, the sun is almost setting and you must be to bed. You three boys are to sleep in the guest chamber and Tobias may share with you."

"Oh, all right," said Nathaniel. "Come on we will show you."

The boys started to walk back to the castle, leaving Rebekah with Zio.

"Good night," called the dragon after them.

****

The bedroom, the boys discovered, was at the top of one of the towers and overlooked the surrounding countryside. The room was round with tapestries hanging from the walls. Four small oak beds stood around the walls with a small chest to the left of each of them and a chair on the right sides. A gentle fire burned in a grate keeping the room warm. Each bed was covered with blankets of animal skins with a large tapestry of a hunting party hanging on the wall. In the corner of the room (if round rooms can have a corner) there was a large oak cupboard with a jug of water and a large bowl standing on it. Timothy looked at it.

"How am I supposed to get a drink from that bowl?" he asked.

Tobias looked at him and shook his head. "That is for washing in not drinking. There are glasses by your beds with water to drink."

"Oh yes, I knew that," said Timothy.

All four boys found that they were rather sleepier than they had realized. They lay down one by one but continued talking to each other. It did not take long for Tobias to discover that no one was answering him as he spoke. He sat up and looked around. Robert lay on his back snoring gently. Timothy and Michael lay on their sides one to the left and one to the right. Tobias smiled to himself. He wondered how his new friends would cope when they found out the truth about him; the boys were in for a big surprise. The boy lay back wondering when he would tell them his secret and as he thought Tobias slowly drifted off to sleep.

Outside the door, the servant sent by the Queen to check on the boys lay dying in a pool of blood. Baron Blackheart was wiping his dagger on the servant's clothes, waiting until he was sure that the boys were asleep.

10

Robert was the first to wake; slowly he opened his eyes and saw Timothy to his left still sleeping soundly. Tobias was to his right and was just starting to wake. Robert got out of bed and found in the chest beside him there were some clothes like the ones that Tobias wore. Tobias was out of bed next and, after a lot of giggling, he showed Robert how to put on the strange clothes. All the noise woke Timothy, and for once he also got up quickly finding the same strange clothes in his chest. The three boys looked to the bed Michael had been sleeping in, it was empty.

"He must have got up and gone for a walk," said Robert. "He often does that at home."

The boys played quietly in their room waiting for Michael to return, but after half an hour Timothy's tummy decided it was time for food so Tobias suggested that they went down for breakfast.

When the boys opened the door of their room all three let out a gasp, for there in the doorway lay the dead servant. Robert screamed, and then thought of his younger brother.

"MICHAEL!" he shouted at the top of his voice. Michael did not come, but a guard who was stationed at the bottom of the tower did. He came up the stairs as fast as he could. The guard was also shocked, but tried not to show it. All thoughts of food had gone from the boys' minds; all they were thinking about now was Michael.

The guard took charge. "All right boys, step over the body and we will go down and find your brother." He turned to Tobias for some help. The boy suddenly realized that as a King's ward he was expected to do something, and the trouble was he just did not know what to do. So instead he was the first to step over the servant and make his way down the stairs, the others following. Tobias felt sick and he hoped that they were not going to find Michael lying dead somewhere.

Down in the main hall there were guards everywhere, all rushing about trying to look as if they knew what they were doing. None of them saw the three boys enter the room. Robert overheard one of them saying something about a note being found, but he could not be sure what it was about. At the end of the room there was a lot of commotion as the King entered, still in his nightclothes. A trumpeter sounded a long blast and everyone fell quiet. The King held aloft a small piece of paper and with his voice shaking with rage he began to speak.

"I have here a demand from Baron Blackheart and his followers, which was pinned to the door of my bed chamber by a bloodied dagger. I have one week to hand over the throne of England to Blackheart and declare him King or the child he has taken as a hostage will die."

Timothy could not contain himself. "NO!" he shouted at the top of his voice, running to the King. He fell to his knees in front of the King. "Please," he begged, "please don't let them hurt my brother."

The crowd of people in the hall saw the King do something he had never done before. Right in front of his subjects the King got down on one knee and put his arm round Timothy. The child threw himself into the King's arms and started to sob. No one in the room moved or spoke; they just allowed the King and this small stranger time to hug. After what seemed like an age the King stood, still holding Timothy's hand. Turning to his left he beckoned to a guard. "Mobilize my army, we are going to war." Then turning to the rest of the people gathered in the Great Hall he said, "We will not rest until Michael is returned to his brothers and they are able to go to their own home and be reunited with their father. Go, gather what weapons you can, we will defeat this evil Baron and have peace in this land. I will never give up the throne of England for a baron."

There was a cheer and all the people in the room started to leave to fetch from their homes whatever weapons they had. Robert could only think of the note the King had read out, was he the only one to remember the threat to kill his brother? Robert bit his lip as he fought back the tears; no one was going to see him cry in public. No one did, but only because Robert ran from the room, followed by Tobias.

Tobias found Robert sitting on the stairs leading up to their room; Robert's shoulders were going up and down and he was rocking silently from side to side. Tobias sat on the stair next to him and put his arm round him. Robert sank into Tobias and sobbed his heart out. The two boys just sat there, one crying for his lost brother and the other trying to comfort his friend, but not sure how to. After a few minutes there was a slight cough and looking up the boys saw the Queen kneeling down in front of them.

"Please come with me," she said, as she held out her hands. The boys stood and Robert, with tears still running down his face, was led by the Queen into a part of the castle only the royal family was allowed to enter. Tobias followed.

They went through a grand oak door that was guarded by a knight on each side. Both guards bowed low as the Queen and the boys approached. Once inside the room the boys found themselves in a small but warm room. Tapestries of hunting scenes hung from the walls and a roaring fire was in the grate. Sitting around the fire were the King and the other children. Timothy stood by the window looking out. As they entered the King stood and gently led Timothy to the fire.

"Children," the King spoke softly, "never in all the years that I have ruled this country have I come across anyone who could do something so low or so evil as to take a child as a hostage. I promise you that I will not rest until your brother is found. You came here by ways that none of us understand, and you are here to help me, now it is my turn to help you. We will find Michael and if he has been hurt, or worse, the evil Blackheart will never be able to flee from me and my army. We will hunt him down to the edge of the world."

11

Michael woke with a start; a heavy hand was shaking him awake. As he slowly came round he wondered why he had the worst headache he had ever had. It felt as if someone was sitting on his chest and hitting his head with a large hammer. He could hear a voice echo inside his head, but could not understand what was being said. Then the voice gradually became clear.

"Come on get up, you little pest."

The hands were shaking him harder.

"What? Where? My head hurts."

"Shut up and eat this."

Slowly the room stopped going round in Michael's head and slowly came into focus. It had cold, bare walls and Michael shivered in the cold. He was lying on dirty straw that had been thrown on the floor, under a rough blanket that had been thrown over him. As he tried to get up from the floor, Michael stumbled and as he fell back down he tipped the food on himself and the floor. The voice laughed, "Oh well, you will have to go hungry then."

The door to the room slammed shut. He heard a heavy clunk as the door was locked. He was trapped but he was sure he had recognized the voice, but he could not remember who it was.

****

Duncan slowly opened his master's door.

"Sire, I have a message from the dungeon guard, your guest has knocked over the food and he can be heard crying. The guard asks what he should do."

"Do?" stormed Blackheart. "He should do nothing. If that little brat starves himself to death at least I won't have to worry about how to get rid of him."

"As you wish master," groveled the servant. He backed out of the room, bowing as he went. "Sorry to have interrupted you."

"Wait, call the region's barons, I want to see them this evening, I have good news for them."

Duncan nodded and was gone.

That evening the barons arrived, and after they were all in the Great Hall Blackheart entered from behind a curtain.

"Welcome my friends! I have great news. One of the children has been captured and as we speak is in the dungeon of this castle. So far the little monster has refused to eat so hopefully he will starve himself to death, then, at least, we will be rid of one of them."

There was a murmur of satisfaction from the back of the room. No one had noticed that a large man had entered the room. Blackheart called to his closest ally.

"Tregore, come and tell us what is going on at the soon-to-be-ex-king's castle."

Tregore went and stood next to the Baron.

"Well," he began, "the kingdom is in chaos, the King has mobilized the whole army and the peasants have been sent to gather whatever they have that can be used as a weapon. The King said that he would not rest until you are found and the boy is returned to his brothers."

There was a slight murmur as some of the knights and barons assembled in the Great Hall realized for the first time that they were going to have to fight.

Blackheart held up his hand, and at once the room was silent.

"We have nothing to fear from the King and his followers. Some of us may die but those of us who are left will control the whole country and be rich. The peasants will do all our hard work for us or they will be executed." The baron looked sideways at Tregore who smiled. "I intend to make all those who are loyal to me richer than you can imagine and those who do not support me… well, there won't be any who don't support me as they will be all dead!"

A cheer went up from the assembled crowd.

There was a slight disturbance from the back of the hall and a man stepped forward.

"I am the Earl of Bristol and although I agree with removing the King from power I do not, however, believe in killing children. Is there not another way we can defeat the King?"

Blackheart called the Earl forward and put his arm round the man's shoulder.

"What other ways do you suggest?"

The Earl looked at the Baron.

"Well, I'm not sure, I haven't thought about…"

"I thought not," said the Baron and he silently drew his dagger and without a word plunged it into the Earl's heart.

The man fell dead without a sound.

"Does anyone else have anything to say?"

The room was silent.

****

Michael jumped; he had felt something crawl across his face, and as he reached up to brush it away a rat scurried into the corner. Michael was cold and very hungry, he was not sure how long he had been in the dungeon but it felt like weeks. He got up and by the light that was filtering in through a small barred window high up in the wall he surveyed his surroundings. The door was in the wall opposite the window and had a small grille in it. In the corner there was a small cracked jug containing dirty water for him to drink. Next to it was a pot for him to use as his toilet. He shuddered. As he looked around Michael became aware that he was being watched, he looked up and saw a face at the door. He heard a bolt in the door slide back, and into the room stepped Tregore.

"Tregore! I am so glad you have come. Has the King sent you to free me?"

Tregore snorted and pushed the boy to the floor.

"Tregore?" Michael looked at his friend, confused.

"The King thinks I work for him, but he is wrong, I work for the great Baron Blackheart. He will free us from the King's power."

"But what will become of me and my brothers?" Michael asked, with tears in his eyes.

"You will die of course! I am looking forward to my axe slicing through your neck, and the necks of your brothers followed by those of the royal family," Tregore said, laughing. He put a bowl of stew on the floor and a crust of moldy bread and, as he left, Michael saw a smile spread across his face.

Michael dropped to the ground and with his fingers stuffed the food into his mouth. He could feel the maggots from the bread crawl around his tongue before he swallowed them and was almost sick. Somewhere in the back of his mind he heard his father tell him to wash his hands before he ate, but try as he might he could not remember what his father looked like. He could only remember his father tucking him into bed at night with a kiss and telling him that he loved him. As Michael lay on the cold damp straw he allowed the tears to come, slowly at first then in a rush as he cried for his dad.

12

Zio the dragon did not feel well he had turned a horrid shade of gray. His cold was getting worse and now he had a headache. As he sat in the corner of his stable he felt left out. He knew that something was wrong; he had heard people rushing about all morning.

"It's not fair," he muttered. "I know that no one thinks that I am important, but they could at least bring me my breakfast."

Slowly he got up from the floor and waddled over to the door and looked out. None of the stable workers seemed to be around. As he watched, Zio saw more and more people making their way to the castle, and all of them carried some sort of weapon. Some were carrying bows while others had swords. Even the peasants had found farming tools or whatever they could.

"Excuse me," said Zio to a guard as he ran past, "what is going on?"

The guard stopped and went up to the dragon.

"Baron Blackheart has taken one of the young visitors as a hostage and is giving the King one week to hand over the throne or the child will die."

The guard hurried on his way.

"WHAT!" roared Zio, smoke trickling out of his nostrils. The dragon forgot his cold and headache he turned red with anger no one was going to hurt one of the children while he was around. Zio called after the guard but he hurried on not hearing. By carefully using his tail Zio reached out and slipped the bolt back and eased the door open.

In all the commotion no one seemed to notice him as he hurried to the castle. He had to duck as he went in through the big oak door, but he still managed to catch the end of his tail between the door and the wall. Zio came to a sudden halt and a peasant tripped and fell over his outstretched tail. "Sorry," the dragon muttered, as he unhooked his tail and the peasant got up.

The guard at the entrance to the Great Hall was barring the way in. "No dragons allowed in the Great Hall."

Zio looked at him and with a gentle puff the guard's beard went up in smoke. The guard dropped his lance as he grabbed his face. Zio walked into the room and as he went his tail clipped the guard whose beard was on fire and sent him crashing to the floor.

Four guards rushed to stop Zio entering the room, but when they noticed the slow trickle of smoke coming from his nose they stopped and looked at the King. The whole room fell silent. No one had ever seen the dragon enter the Great Hall before. The King thought for a moment, let out a sigh and putting his hand up to the guards said, "Let him in, the whole castle is in chaos; a dragon in the Great Hall will not make a lot of difference."

Robert, Timothy, Rebekah, Tobias, Nathaniel and Adam all walked up to the dragon. Nathaniel and Adam had bows across their shoulders and each had a bag of arrows at their hips. Robert put his hand out and touched the scaly back of Zio and quietly under his breath he said, "Thank you for coming."

The dragon looked at the boy and put his arm around his shoulders.

"I need to be here."

And turning to the King Zio announced to all in the room, "I will do whatever you ask to free this boy's brother Your Majesty."

"Thank you, Zio, but I do not know what good a dragon will be."

The King addressed the crowd assembled before him.

"As you all know, Robert and Timothy's brother Michael has been kidnapped and he is under threat of death. I have sworn to the children that I will not rest until the young lad has been found and returned to his brothers. I made a promise that these children would be given the rights of a King's ward. Robert and Timothy please approach the throne."

Timothy and Robert looked at each other not sure what was expected of them. Tobias shook his head and putting his hands on the shoulders of his new friends he gently led them up to the King. The crowd laughed as the three small boys walked right up to the King and Robert held out his hand. The King took it and shook it solemnly, ignoring the fact that just a few days ago if anyone had failed to bow as they approached the King they would have been beheaded. The boys saw a small cushion in the hands of a guard standing to the left of the King and slightly behind him. The King nodded to the guard who stepped smartly forward. On the cushion the boys could see two golden-handled daggers with white pointed blades. There was a space where a third had been. The King took one of the daggers and attached it to Robert's belt. He did the same with Timothy.

The daggers felt heavy on their belts and as the boys adjusted the daggers they felt pleasant electric tingles go through their bodies.

"Wow! What was that?" Timothy asked.

No one answered but a few in the crowd gave each other a knowing glance. The King also smiled but said nothing; he knew all would be explained in time.

Robert noticed the space on the cushion where Michael's dagger would have been but he bit his lip and said nothing in case he upset Timothy. King Christian addressed the crowd.

"Don't forget that these boys are royal wards, and as such are under my protection. All who help them help the kingdom, but if any one hinders them in their quest to find the crown of England or their brother the punishment will be death."

A cheer went up from the crowd. No one had heard Tregore snort, but just in case they did Tregore managed to turn it into a sort of cough. He had arrived as the boys had gone up to receive their daggers.

"Tregore," the King beckoned to the axe man. "Yes sire?" Tregore replied, as he approached the throne.

"Tregore, as you are one of my most trusted aides I am making you responsible for these children. If anything happens to them you will be personally accountable to me. You will move out of your cottage in the woods and live in the cottage inside the castle walls by the keep".

Tregore started to argue but thought better of it; he would have to see what his master Baron Blackheart wanted him to do.

"At once sire. May I be permitted to have the children stay with me where I can keep an eye on them?"

"No, they will stay in the castle where my guards will keep watch day and night. Now go and gather your possessions. I expect you to be living here by nightfall."

Tregore bowed low and left the castle, smiling to himself. It would now be a lot easier to kill the children.

Robert felt a shiver run down his spine at the thought of Tregore, but he was not sure why.

Zio, who had been sitting at the back of the hall, sneezed. The tapestry that had been hanging near to him was suddenly engulfed in flames.

"Sorry," Zio apologized.

When a fire-breathing dragon sneezes, a small ball of flame shoots out of his nose and sets fire to whatever it lands on.

Zio wiped his nose on his tail, and as his tail whipped back behind him he caught Tobias across the back of the shoulders and sent him sprawling across the floor.

"Sorry," repeated Zio.

"Zio, will you please be careful," shouted the King, "or I will have to ask you to leave."

The dragon had been thinking. Slowly he waddled forward, his tail swishing from side to side. People dived for cover and most got out of the way but one guard was not quick enough and the tip of the tail sent his helmet flying down the Great Hall and through a window. A cry from below the castle informed all inside that the helmet had hit someone walking past.

"Your Majesty, I have been thinking and I have come up with a plan that might be able to get the young boy back."

The King put his hand up to stop the laughter that had drowned out the dragon.

"We will hear what the dragon has to say." Turning to Zio he said,

"I have never had a dragon as an adviser before, but since I banished Blackheart I have been looking for a new one."

Zio approached the throne.

"Sire, Michael has been kidnapped by Baron Blackheart and taken prisoner and the Baron is threatening to kill him, is that right?"

"Yes."

"Well, how would it be if I were to fly to the Baron's castle in the middle of the night and see if I can find him? I can get there quicker than anyone on a horse and no one will see or hear me."

For the first time in a long time the King was speechless. He looked at the Queen for help but she just shrugged her shoulders. King Christian looked round the rest of the room; everyone was looking at him waiting for the King's wisdom.

"Er, that sounds like a very good idea," said the King, wishing he had thought of it.

Robert stepped forward.

"Sir," he began, "I think it is a splendid idea, but I want to go with him so that I know that my brother is still alive."

"Me too," piped up Timothy.

The King hated making decisions, and now he had to make two. Robert and Timothy waited, everyone in the Great Hall waited. The King scratched his head then turned to the assembled crowd.

"Right, this is my order. Zio you will fly to Baron Blackheart's castle tonight to see if you can rescue Michael. Robert and Timothy you will go with him to make sure that he rescues the right boy."

No one saw Tobias as he quietly slipped out of the room. All eyes were on Robert, Timothy and the dragon.

Tobias had to be quick, he had work to do and he needed to contact someone urgently.

"I'm hungry," said Timothy.

13

Michael woke, he was cold and hungry and he could still feel the tears that had stained his face. As he tried to move he heard the door open. Blackheart and Tregore entered the room.

"So you are the little brat who thinks you can save the King." Blackheart laughed. "No one can save you or the King. He must hand the throne over to me by the end of the week or Tregore will have the pleasure of chopping off your head!"

The Baron turned to Tregore.

"When the throne is mine, kill this little pest anyway. It will let the peasants know that they will have to obey me or face the consequences!"

It was Tregore's turn to laugh. He bent down and took Michael's face in his hand. Michael tried to pull away but the fingers of Tregore's hand held his face so hard that he could not speak. Suddenly Michael felt very small and the man seemed very tall and his breath stank as if he had not cleaned his teeth for a month.

"Boy, I think you need to know that your brothers are to be my responsibility, the King has told me to look after them. By this time tomorrow you will all be dead. You will never see your father again!"

Blackheart took something from behind his back; Michael could not quite see what it was.

"I think the time has come to use this," he said, handing Tregore a long chain.

Tregore took it from his master and jangled it in the boy's face, laughing. Michael shrunk away in fear, scared that he might be beaten to death. Blackheart grabbed the boy and threw him on to his front. Michael could feel the warm blood as it oozed from his nose. Tregore quickly bound his feet and locked the end of the chain into a ring on the wall.

"Now, even if we leave the door unlocked, you can't get out! You will die forgotten and alone, you will never be saved, your body will rot and never be found, no one knows where you are!"

Both men left the dungeon laughing cheerfully. As they left the Baron threw a lump of moldy bread back over his shoulder towards Michael.

"We could not have you die hungry, could we?"

The chain dug deep into Michael's legs, and the bread was almost out of reach. And as he stretched for the food the pain was so strong that Michael bit his bottom lip to stop himself crying.

Michael devoured the bread; it felt as though he had not eaten for days. As he ate he could hear his father's words in his ears.

"No matter what people try to do, Good will ALWAYS win, never forget that."

Michael did not cry, he decided that he would never cry again. If he was to die he knew that he would die bravely. The small child huddled himself in the corner as far away from the door as the chain would allow. He tried to remember what his father looked like, but the more he tried to remember the more he could see Tregore's face laughing at him. The boy curled himself into a ball and shivered, waiting for death.

At the top of Michael's cell wall was a small barred window and if he had been able to climb up and look out to he would have heard huge wings beating and in the distance and he would have seen the shape of Zio fly across the face of the moon. Michael could not reach the window because of the chains and even if he had, the undergrowth outside was too thick to see through. All he could hear now were rats squeaking as they fought over the crumbs of the moldy bread that he had dropped and his own heart beating in his chest.

****

Timothy and Robert hung on to the ends of a leather strap that Zio had round his shoulders. Neither boy spoke as each was terrified and was hanging on as if their lives depended on it, which they did. Robert was thinking about his younger brother and hoping he was still alive. He also plotted in his mind what he would do to Blackheart if he had killed him. Timothy was also thinking about his twin, while he bit into the chicken leg that he had brought with him.

Zio (who now had turned himself black so as not to be seen in the night) flew like he had never flown before; he could see the Baron's castle below but flew on. He knew that to land too close would be dangerous. And he would have to be as careful as he could be with two noisy boys with him. He could still taste the revolting mixture that one of the King's maids had made him drink before he left the castle. She told him that it would stop him sneezing. He had stopped sneezing but he wished it had tasted better.

"Hold tight boys; we are going to land in that wood over on the left." As he spoke Zio dipped his left wing and went down fast and silently.

Timothy gasped, "It's like being on a roller coaster, only higher!"

"And scarier!" shouted Robert.

Before they knew what had happened they were on the ground and both boys tumbled off the back of the dragon. Robert picked himself up and dusted himself down. Timothy was looking among the tree roots.

"Wish I had got a torch."

"What have you dropped?" both the dragon and Robert asked.

"My chicken leg." muttered Timothy.

"Right boys, sit down, there is something I need to tell you."

The boys sat down.

"There are a few things that you need to know about. The King gave you each a dagger and told you that you are royal wards. Robert, reach up and feel the harness around the top of my head."

Robert did so.

"Do you feel a small pouch?"

Robert nodded.

"Good, that is your brother's dagger for when we get him

out of the Baron's castle. The daggers are magic; the handle is gold and the blade is a dragon tooth."

Both boys gasped.

"Dragon magic is not like other magic, it can only be used for good. The daggers can only be used to defend yourself or a friend or to do good. You must never use a dagger in anger. If you ever use them to attack they will shatter and dissolve. You will find out how to use them properly as time goes on."

"There is something else you need to know," a voice said from the darkness.

The boys turned to the direction of the voice. Out from the undergrowth stepped Tobias.

"Hello."

"Tobias, how did you get here," Robert began, "and what do you mean there's something else we need to know?"

Tobias smiled. "I also come from the future, your future."

14

The Baron had been busy; while his henchmen had been guarding the boy in the dungeon he had sent riders out far and wide to get together all the barons, lords and their soldiers who he knew would stand with him in a fight. In the grounds of his castle he had an army of over 3,000. Easily enough to overthrow the King and his small army. Blackheart smiled to himself as he again thought of how naive the King was to think that everybody loved him.

Tregore had been sent back to the castle and told to move into the castle cottage and be ready to kill the boys and the royal family.

Duncan scurried into the Baron's private quarters.

"Sir."

"Have I not told you to never come into these rooms without being summoned?" Blackheart turned and with the back of his hand he hit Duncan in the face. The servant fell crashing to the floor. Duncan got up, brushed himself down and addressed his master.

"Sire, the Lord Nordelph wishes to speak with you."

"Show him in then."

A knight in shining armor walked in, he was tall and he had a long red cape hanging from his shoulders. As he entered he bowed his head and hit his chest with his fist.

"Sire, it is a great pleasure to serve under your command to rid England of this soft King. I look forward to seeing his head on a spike above this castle."

"Yes, yes very nice of you to grovel to me but what news do you have for me?"

"Sire, it is with great pleasure I tell you the army is now ready. When do we march?"

The Baron stood and went to the window. Down below in the courtyard he could see row upon row of soldiers many of whom had flaming torches held high. Blackheart smiled.

"Now! We will be at the King's castle by dawn and at noon the throne will be mine!"

The Baron swept from the room followed by Lord Nordelph and Duncan.

****

The King was having a bad night; he had doubled the guard round his family and had insisted that the children sleep in the adjoining room to him and the Queen. That left just over 500 knights around the rest of the castle along with all the peasants that he could find to protect his kingdom. The King knew that he had been foolish to keep such a small army, but he had never felt the need of more soldiers, until now. As he paced up and down in his room he suddenly felt as if someone had joined him in the room. He drew the short dagger he always kept up his sleeve and turning he raised his arm to strike. He dropped the dagger as before him stood his daughter Rebekah. Rebekah bent down and picked up the dagger and handed it to her father as if nothing had happened.

"I think you dropped this Father."

The King took it and tucked it out of sight back up his

sleeve.

Rebekah gently took her father by the hand and led him to the window. The moon was full and it lit up the surrounding countryside.

"Look Father, the world is at peace, all the land is yours no one is going to take it from you. As far as you can see there is nothing moving, only the wild animals. Zio is a very clever dragon and I am sure that he will be able to save Michael and bring him back. Then everyone can help you find the crown and all will be back to normal."

As the two of them turned from the window the first of the Baron's army could just be seen coming over the far hill, but neither King Christian nor Rebekah saw them. Nathaniel and Adam, however, had seen them from their window. The two boys looked at each other and without saying a word they picked up their bows and arrows and put them by the window and watched and waited. In the room next door the King went back to bed and the Queen muttered in her sleep but did not wake. Rebekah went through an archway and down a heavily guarded passage back to her own room.

****

As the King and his family woke a few short hours later the sun was streaming in through their windows showing all that morning had come. The door to the royal rooms burst open and Sir Baignard rushed in.

"Sire, the Baron has amassed an army and they are here!"

The King let out a sigh and went to the window with the Queen. The sight that confronted them took them by surprise, during the night Blackheart had moved his army and now ringed the castle. As they watched a single rider rode out towards the castle and on the top of his lance was a white flag.

"They are sending an emissary to offer a peaceful solution," said the Queen. "You had better go and see what they are offering."

"Yes dear," said the King, as he went to get dressed.

****

Robert and Timothy looked at Tobias while they tried to make sense of what he had just told them.

"What do you mean, you come from our future? I thought that you lived here in the King's castle and are a royal ward."

Tobias sat down and motioned for the boys to do the same. Zio sneezed and set fire to the bush that the boys were leaning against.

"Sorry, I think the medicine that I was given is wearing off." As he said it another sneeze set fire to a tree.

"Will you stop that!" said Tobias. "We will be seen."

Timothy asked again, "What do you mean, you come from the future?"

"It is a long story. I was born, sorry, I mean will be born in the year 2130. My parents abandoned me on the day I was born and I was taken in to care. When I was 8 a woman visited and gave me this watch." Tobias moved the sleeve on his left arm to reveal what looked like any ordinary watch.

Robert and Timothy sat open-mouthed; Zio sat quietly in

70

the corner, he already knew the story that Tobias was going to share.

Tobias continued, "I never get a choice of where or when I am to travel. My watch alarm suddenly bleeps and I have only a few short minutes before I am whisked backwards or forwards in time."

"Where have you been?" asked Robert.

"All over the place, the best by far though is this."

"Why?" asked Timothy.

"Because I met you."

"Oh."

Tobias was going to go on but suddenly Robert grabbed his arm and pointed towards the castle. All thought of Tobias's time traveling was taken from their minds as three children and a dragon watched the biggest army that any of them had ever seen stream out of Blackheart's castle and head towards the coast and the King.

"So, it has started," the dragon said.

"What has started?" asked Timothy, who had given up looking for his chicken leg and was watching all the men and horses as they marched away.

"War."

15

Michael heard all the commotion, but had no idea what was going on. He could hear people shouting, laughing and more shouting. He remembered how Tregore had hurt his face when he held it in his hand. The bread had tasted foul but it had been better than the pain of hunger. He felt sad that he would never see his brothers or his new friends or his father again, Michael knew that his time was short. He wondered what death would be like, and would it hurt or not? How long would it take? Tregore had talked of chopping off his head and Michael thought that would hurt, a lot.

After what seemed like an age the boy became aware that the castle was silent. He listened, all the shouting had stopped, and there were not even the normal sounds of castle life. All he could hear was his own breathing, the rats as they scurried across the floor and the sounds of his chains as they scraped across the floor when he moved trying to lie more comfortably. Michael pulled himself into the corner of the dungeon, hunched up his knees, put his head on them and waited for it all to end.

****

In the woods not far from Michael, three boys and a dragon sat waiting for the army of Blackheart to disappear from view. All thoughts of how Tobias had come from the future were gone from Robert's mind. All he thought of at the moment was his younger brother and if he was still alive. After what seemed like an age the army could no longer be seen or heard. Zio remembered the King telling him that Blackheart would almost certainly have killed Michael, or left someone with orders to do so. The dragon knew that he would have to tell the boys, but he didn't want the responsibility.

"Boys, come here and sit down, there is something I need to tell you."

The boys sat.

"As you know, before we set off the King took me to one side. Robert, Timothy, it is my duty to tell you that Baron Blackheart has a reputation of not treating his prisoners very well. The King told me to warn you that your brother might have already been hurt, or worse…" His words trailed off as Tobias, without a word, went over to his friends and sat between them.

"What do you mean, or worse?" demanded Timothy.

"I know what you mean," Robert struggled to get the words out, "you mean dead don't you?"

The dragon nodded. Robert got up and went to the edge of the woods and stared into the distance. He said nothing but the tears were making lines in the dirt on his face.

Timothy jumped to his feet.

"If that evil man has hurt my brother I will kill him myself, I swear it." As he spoke his hand tightened round the dagger on his belt. He remembered the dragon's warning that the dagger was for defense only but he didn't care.

Zio decided it was time to take action; all thoughts of his cold had gone. He did not even notice that he had not sneezed for ages.

"Well, there is only one way to find out, let's go and see if he is still alive."

Slowly and carefully, and as quietly as three boys and a dragon could, they made their way towards the outer walls of the castle.

****

King Christian was not happy, he had hated horses ever since he was a child and had fallen off in front of his father and mother and hundreds of guests at his tenth birthday. He had received the pony as a present from a lord who was trying to make peace with the King, his father. The lord and his father had laughed along with the crowd and Christian had never forgotten it. Now he had to get on a horse and go and meet this knight who as bearing a white flag. As the King approached the knight he recognized him as one of the knights who had served him before Blackheart was banished.

"Nordelph, I thought you had more sense than to join up with that treacherous swine Blackheart. Obviously, I was wrong. What terms does you evil master offer?"

Lord Nordelph felt very uncomfortable, he had begged Blackheart to send Tregore instead but the Baron had refused. Instead, he had ordered Tregore back to the King's side to continue acting as a spy in the castle and to be ready to kill the royal family.

"I have been ordered to offer you and your family safe

passage out of this country in return for your throne. I have been told to tell you that my master has the boy Michael and unless you accept this offer the child will be killed. You have one hour to decide or the castle will be attacked and everyone in it will be put to the sword."

Christian looked at the knight in disgust.

"The note that Blackheart left gave me a week."

"Things change."

With that, Lord Nordelph turned his horse and galloped off to join his army. The King turned his horse and at a more sedate pace went back to the castle. As he entered through the gates he nodded to one of the guards to his left and with a low rumble then a loud crash the portcullis came down. The King rode right up to the castle keep before he dismounted, not as neatly as he had hoped, but at least he did not fall off.

"Summon my knights to the Great Hall now.

" The King informed his knights of the Baron's offer. Sir Baignard said what they were all thinking.

"Who does the Baron think he is ordering the King about? Sire, we will defend you and your family until the last drop of blood seeps from our bodies. We will never surrender to that evil man."

There was a murmur of approval from the assembled crowd who beat their shields with their swords. They were eager to get into battle. The King held up his hand and at once the room became silent.

"My friends, we must face facts, we are outnumbered, and although we have enough food and water for a few weeks we cannot hold out for ever. It is useless to sacrifice lives for no reason. I do not trust Blackheart to honor his offer of safe passage to my family and me. I am sure that he means to kill us all."

"Then, sire, we must smuggle you and your family out of the castle and away into the woods." Sir Baignard turned to one of the castle servants. "Go and make ready the secret passage."

The servant bowed to the knight then, forgetting to bow to his King, he hurried from the room.

****

Rebekah, Nathaniel and Adam had been listening to the plans made for them from an upper gallery overlooking the Great Hall. Rebekah looked at her brothers.

"We must do whatever father asks of us, he and his knights will keep mother and us safe from the Baron."

Nathaniel and Adam looked at each other and nodded. The two princes and the princess made their way to the top of the castle to a hidden room. This room was kept secret by the King for just such an emergency as this. In the room the children found clothes that were old and scruffy. Slowly they changed into them. The King had told them when he first lost the crown that if the castle ever came under attack they were to change into peasant clothing and go and find the one person the King trusted above all others. They would then be smuggled out as servant children and be kept hidden until it was safe to return to the castle.

The King met his children halfway down the hidden stairway.

"Well done children. Come, let us find our friend and get you away from the castle and into safety."

The children followed their father down into the cellar where the cook had moved a chest away from the wall; behind it there was a small trapdoor in the floor that led to the secret passage and freedom.

"Ah, there you are," said the King. "Please take the royal children and hide them in the woods as we have agreed."

"At once sire," said Tregore, as he held open the trapdoor for the children.

16

Zio and the boys arrived at the base of the castle walls by using as much of the undergrowth to hide in as they could. They all felt sure that there would be guards on the towers ready to rain down arrows and crossbow bolts upon them. Once they were against the walls they made their way round to where the dungeon was. It was easy to find because when the castle had been built the dungeons had been put outside the main wall. Robert was the first to get there.

"I've found it," he called to the others, and beckoned them over. Tobias started to look around at the bottom of the wall.

"What are you looking for?" asked Timothy.

"There should be a small window with bars on it to allow light and air into the prison cell. There is just too much undergrowth to find it."

"Let me be of help," said Zio, and carefully the dragon got as close to the ground as he could and slowly breathed out a small flame which turned the bushes to cinders in moments.

"Just like dad's blowtorch!" exclaimed Timothy.

Down below Michael woke. The chains had dug deep into his flesh and blood was seeping onto the floor. He tried to move but was too stiff to do so. He could smell burning and wondered what it was. He was still not sure whether he was dead or alive when he heard his name being called.

"Michael, Michael are you down there?"

Michael thought that he must be dead and the voice calling him was an angel, but he could not work out why it sounded like his brother. Suddenly the room got brighter as Zio incinerated bushes next to the window.

"Down here," Michael called out, his voice sounding weak and gravelly, realizing for the first time that he was not dead. "Down here."

Timothy let out a whoop of delight.

"We've found him! Michael we're coming to save you! Hold on."

Tobias shook the bars; they were stuck fast into the wall.

"We will never get them out," he sighed.

Zio said nothing; he just lay on the ground and got his face as close to the window as he could. When he felt he was close enough he took a deep breath and blew an intense bright blue flame out of the end of his nose. Slowly he moved his face backwards and forwards across the bars, melting the iron. The boys stood back and watched, all glad that they had a friend that could do that. Timothy was thinking how much he would like to take him to school and sort out the class bully.

Clang! The first bar hit the dungeon floor, followed shortly after by the last two. The noise had not gone unnoticed and while the three boys and Zio watched, the door to Michael's cell opened and in walked Duncan with a long sharp sword. Robert saw the Baron's servant from the small window high above and pushing past Zio he shouted through the window, "If you hurt my brother I will find you and kill you!"

Duncan walked over to the cowering Michael, and ignoring the shouts from above he gently moved Michael away from the wall. The boys at the window could only watch as he went to the wall and using his sword started to chip at the cement holding Michael's chain. After what seemed like an age the chain came away from the wall and fell on the floor. Michael bit his lip to fight the pain. Duncan looked down at the small, dirty and smelly child at his feet.

"So you are the one who has been getting my master angry. I hear that you are going to find King Christian's crown, I pray that you can."

Looking up at the window he beckoned to the others.

"Come down, I won't hurt you."

The boys were not sure, they looked at Zio.

"You might as well, if he had wanted to hurt you he could have killed Michael, but he hasn't has he?"

The dragon turned round and let his tail down through the window into the cell below. Timothy was the first one down. He grabbed on to the tail and slid all the way down. He had to drop the last few feet, as Zio's tail was not quite long enough. Picking himself up from the floor he charged over to his twin and threw himself at him. Michael cried out in pain. Timothy stood back and for the first time the boy noticed how weak his brother looked. The entire color had gone from his skin. Timothy remembered looking at some old parchment in a museum with his father, his brother's skin reminded him of it. He wondered if this was what old people looked like when they were dead. By the time Tobias and Robert had slid down the tail, Duncan had carefully untied the chains from Michael's legs. Robert was nearly sick; the smell from the wound was awful. Puss was oozing from Michael's leg and maggots were feeding on his rotten flesh.

Zio (who by now had turned round and had his head stuck through the window) called out to the boys, "Robert, use the dagger to cut out the infection, Timothy get hold of your brother's head, and give him something to bite on to." The boys moved to obey. Timothy knelt with his knees one each side of Michael's head and he placed the hilt if his dagger in between his brothers teeth. Robert took hold of his feet, and Tobias held his friend's hand to comfort him.

"Wait!" called Duncan and he left the room to return seconds later with an old cloth that he placed under the boy's head.

"Do it," said Zio.

Robert bit his lip and with a lump in his throat he started to cut. Michael wriggled, as the pain was unbearable. Timothy noticed that his brother had bitten so hard onto the hilt of the dagger his mouth had started to bleed. As Robert cut his brother's leg with the dragon tooth dagger there was a hissing noise and the smell of burning flesh. The tears from Timothy fell on his brother and cooled his face and Robert carried on cutting away. Slowly Michael's wriggling stopped and with a sigh he collapsed.

"You have killed him!" shouted Timothy and he got up and started hitting his older brother. Robert did not fight back.

"STOP THAT AT ONCE!"

Timothy stopped mid-fight and turned to face Zio who had smoke trickling out of his nostrils.

"Robert, listen to me, you must trust me. Keep cutting away the dead flesh. Timothy, hold your brother's head like you were."

The boys looked at Tobias who nodded and they went back to their work. Robert started on Michael's second leg, the hissing seemed worse than it had on the first leg and the maggots were blood-red and fat from all the rotten flesh that they had been eating. But this time the boy did not wriggle or cry out. Duncan, without speaking, put his hand on Timothy's shoulder as the boy cried for his brother. Robert stood up, blood dripping from his dagger. Timothy shook his twin to try to wake him, but Michael remained motionless. Duncan gently moved the boys away from Michael and picked the child up. Michael's body hung limp in his arms. Duncan looked at Zio and shook his head. Robert looked at the dagger in his hand and dropped it as if it had burnt him. Tobias went to his new friend and without speaking put his arm around him.

Timothy went up to Duncan and started hitting him.

"No, no, no, don't let him die."

Duncan, without a word, knelt and put the lifeless Michael on the floor. He looked at Timothy.

"I'm sorry son," was all the servant could say.

Timothy slid to the floor and hung on to Duncan. As the tears fell he knew that his brother who he shared everything with was dead.

17

Rebekah was very happy, she had been friends with Tregore all her life and she, like her father, trusted him. The passage had led them into the woods not far from Tregore's cottage and she and her brothers knew that their father and mother would follow them and soon they all would be together and safe. What the royal children had not noticed, however, was as they emerged from the tunnel Tregore had pulled a hidden lever and after a low rumble the roof of the passage had collapsed, blocking the entrance at the castle. The King and Queen were trapped. Nathaniel and Adam ran along happily playing and looking forward to spending time in Tregore's cottage in the woods.

After what seemed like only a few minutes they arrived at Tregore's cottage. Rebekah was the first to notice it.

"I can see light coming from your home, but you have not been living there for ages, who can it be?"

Tregore said nothing, he just ushered the children towards the door.

"Hey, don't push, I am a prince after all," Nathaniel demanded.

Tregore just grunted and as he did so Baron Blackheart walked out of Tregore's door.

"Welcome, children, welcome to the end of the world as you know it! Soon you and those other children will all be dead. And I will be King!"

The children tried to run but the fat man barred their way.

"Tregore, how could you? My father trusted you with everything and you repay him like this," Rebekah shouted, hitting the man she had up to now called a friend.

Tregore just laughed. "I have spent too many years serving under your father as a paid servant. That will never happen again. Before long England will have a new King, Blackheart, and I will serve as his equal."

The Baron smiled to himself but said nothing.

The royal children were pushed into the cottage and were bound hand and foot.

"You will be dead in a few short hours, and the kingdom will be mine!" Blackheart laughed as the children were pushed into the corner of the cottage.

****

The King's castle was in uproar, the time had nearly run out for the King to answer the offer put to him by Nordelph and everyone was making ready for battle. The King and his wife had dressed as peasants and were making their way to the castle kitchens to follow the children and Tregore. Sir Baignard met them as they entered the room.

"Sire, there has been an accident, the roof of the secret passage has collapsed and you cannot get out. As soon as it was noticed I sent one of the serving wenches to the tower and she reports that the children and Tregore were seen running to cover amongst the trees."

Gwendolyn let out a sigh.

"At least the children are safe."

She was interrupted by a long trumpet blast that sounded from outside the castle. A knight came running and fell at the King's feet.

"Sire, you had better come quickly, Baron Blackheart is at the entrance with a white flag, and he demands to see you."

"How dare he demand that my husband does anything," began the Queen, but with a wave of his hand the King silenced her.

"Let us see what he wants, though I don't imagine he has come to surrender."

The King, with two of his most trusted knights, made his way to the portcullis where two knights stood barring Blackheart's way. The King, checking that the portcullis was firmly locked down, beckoned Blackheart to approach.

"What do you want, you scoundrel? I should have had you executed when I had the chance."

"Your Majesty," began the Baron bowing low, "I am here to receive your answer. Will you hand over the throne to me or do you wish to have all your household and family put to the sword?"

"I will never give in to a tyrant who threatens me, or my family. You do have a bigger army than me and you might beat me in a fight, but my children are safe and out of the castle. In time they will raise up an army and wipe you out."

Blackheart smiled.

"Let me introduce you to my second in command."

The Baron made a slight wave of his hand and Tregore stepped into view, leading a horse with three very scared and tightly bound royal children sitting backwards on it.

"You were saying, Your Majesty?"

18

Michael was dead. His brothers felt numb. Tobias did not know what to feel. He had never had a friend die before, let alone in front of him. Zio, with his head still poking through the window, spoke to Duncan.

"Is there anyone else in the castle? Are we safe to move the body?"

Duncan suddenly came to his senses; for what seemed like an age he had been looking at the child's lifeless body at his feet. As he looked at Michael a plan was forming itself in his mind. Duncan had known long ago that he would kill Blackheart, but now his resolve grew stronger. He looked up at the dragon.

"I was left here with instructions to kill the boy; I no longer need to do that as he is dead. There is no one else here, they have all gone to battle."

Zio nodded.

"Bring the body out to me, we cannot leave him to rot in the dungeon."

Duncan bent down and picked up the child and led the way up a winding stairway and out into the main part of the castle. A sad and silent procession made its way towards the gate. Duncan with Michael in his arms, the boys' head and legs swinging limply as the servant walked. Three small boys walking behind, heads bowed so that no one could see the tears. As they approached the outer wall of the castle

Tobias saw a shovel leaning against the wall and without speaking picked it up. His two friends noticed but said nothing; they all knew it was to dig the grave with. All Robert could think about was what his father would say. With a loud crash the drawbridge came crashing down. Zio stood outside. For the first time the children saw a Zio they had not seen before, one that was serious and in control.

"Bring the boy."

Zio turned and walked towards the woods. Silently the procession followed the dragon.

****

High up in one of the castle towers a knight looked out of a window and watched. He waited until the friends disappeared into the woods, and when he knew the coast was clear the knight went down the stairs and through a hidden door to where his horse was waiting. His master, Baron Blackheart had told him to watch Duncan. The baron had never trusted his groveling servant. The knight made his way towards Tregore's cottage half a night's ride away, where he knew the Baron would be waiting to hear of the child's death.

Lord Hampstead rode as hard as he could. When he arrived the cottage was in darkness, but outside sitting round a fire were two of the servant women from his master's castle. They recognized him at once.

"The Baron has taken the royal children back to their castle; I think he is going to use them to threaten the King," one of the women cackled.

The knight nodded that he understood and turned his

horse towards the king's castle and rode on. As he rode he thought how the Baron would reward him for the wonderful news of Michael's death.

****

The King was speechless and, for the first time ever, so was the Queen. She tried to reach through the portcullis to grab at Tregore. The man she had trusted with the most precious things in the kingdom, their children, had betrayed them.

"Tregore, how could you do this to your King? Wherever you go from now on you will be tracked down, you and Blackheart, and you will be killed, and I will not rest until you are dead."

Tregore laughed.

"I don't think you are in a position to threaten me, you are the one being threatened!"

"Well," demanded Blackheart, "are you going to surrender the throne of England to me? Or are you going to watch your children die?"

"You would not dare to harm the royal children."

"Oh, how wrong you are!"

Turning to Tregore the Baron pointed to a large rock close to the entrance of the castle.

"Do it."

Tregore at once grabbed Rebekah and dragged her off the horse and across to the rock. He threw her across it and waved his arm. At once a page stepped out of the shadows with the executioner's axe. Tregore took it and looked at his master who nodded.

"Father!" Rebekah pleaded.

****

Michael's dead body lay on the ground in a clearing in the wood. Robert, Timothy and Tobias stood round unashamed of their tears. Duncan stood a little away from the others, wishing that he had been man enough to do something to help the boy before it had become too late.

"Right boys, I need you to help me for a minute," said Zio, who was still in charge.

Tobias nodded and picked up the shovel that he had dropped by the entrance to the clearing and slowly, struggling to hold back the tears, started to dig Michael's grave. Duncan quietly walked over to the boy and gently took the shovel from him and continued with the digging. Zio sat down and called the boys over. The three children threw themselves at the dragon and clung to him as if he was their only friend left in the world.

"Boys, I am sorry Michael is dead, but sometimes things that are bad have to happen so better events can follow on. Robert, you trusted me and continued to cut away the rotten flesh even when you knew in your heart of hearts that your brother was dead."

Robert nodded, and wiped his nose on his sleeve.

"Now you will see that the power of good will overcome all evil, as it always does."

"Dad used to say that," Timothy whispered.

"Then your father is a wise man," said Zio. "Now watch to see how good can never be beaten by evil."

The dragon bent down and got his face as close as he could

to the dead boy. Very slowly he breathed in and filled himself with air. As gently as he could he breathed fire into Michael's mouth and nose. Slowly the boy's body started to glow as it became white hot. Robert, Timothy, Tobias and Duncan stood back, the light from Michael's body hurting their eyes. Suddenly there was an ear splitting roar as the light exploded from the body and Zio fell onto his backside. As the three boys, a dragon and an old servant picked themselves up only Zio noticed that Michael was standing up with his hands on his hips. Then suddenly Timothy noticed too and ran at his twin, knocking them both off their feet, followed a few seconds later by Robert and Tobias. Duncan sat stunned on the ground, all he could manage to say was, "Well I'll be! Well I'll be!"

Zio separated the excited boys who were by now rolling around on the ground laughing.

"Boys, boys, boys, you must listen. Michael needs to get his strength back and so do I. It is hard work being dead you know!"

The boys sat down and Timothy walked over to the dragon and threw his arms round the scaly neck.

"Thank you," he whispered.

Robert sat biting his bottom lip.

"Now you have seen dragon magic work." Zio folded his wings around the boys. "It can only be used for good. Michael now has dragon powers, but they will last only a few days."

"What sort of dragon powers?" asked Michael, who was beginning to get his breath back.

"You will not be able to be harmed; if you get hit even by an arrow it will do you no harm. But remember this will not last forever and soon you will be able to be hurt again."

"Wow!" all the boys said together.

"Robert, reach up to the pouch and get your brother's dagger, he might need it."

Robert did as he was told. Michael put the dagger on his belt and stood up. Robert secretly looked at his own dagger, it still had his brother's blood dried on. Robert shivered but said nothing, and he could still remember cutting his brother's legs.

Zio opened a bag that he had been carrying all night.

"Come and eat, we still have a lot of work to do before this night is over"

"Food," exclaimed Timothy and dived at the bag. Then thinking better of it he handed it to his twin. Zio laughed to himself, this was the first time he had seen Timothy pass food on to someone else before stuffing his own mouth.

"Michael you go first, you need to eat more than I do."

Michael smiled and bit into a chicken leg.

After they had all eaten Zio stood up.

"It is time."

"Time for what?" asked Robert.

"Time to show Blackheart that he will never be King!" shouted Tobias as he jumped onto Zio's back. The three brothers followed their friend onto the dragon's back. Duncan was about to leave but Michael held out his hand. Without a word Duncan took it and got up as well.

Zio staggered under the weight but he smiled to himself.

Dragon magic was very powerful. Duncan had been left to kill Michael and here he was being helped up onto his back by Michael himself! No one spoke as the great dragon's wings beat and slowly they all took off into the darkness. They circled the woods a few times gaining height, then slowly Zio turned towards home and a fight.

19

Tregore's axe gleamed in the moonlight as the giant slowly lifted it above his head; time seemed to stand still as everyone watched the axe.

"Wait!" the King shouted.

"Well?" questioned Blackheart.

Rebekah managed to turn her head towards her parents.

"Father, never give up the throne of England for a baron. If I am to die then I will die as a princess not a prisoner!"

The King struggled to speak, but no words would come.

Blackheart turned to Tregore and nodded.

As the axe began to fall there was an ear splitting roar and both Tregore and his axe were consumed in a ball of fire. Zio landed behind the Baron, smoke still trickling from his nose.

The baron's attention was taken off the King for a split second. The King ducked out of his way and, drawing his short dagger faster than any one saw, he reached through the portcullis and stabbed Blackheart in the arm.

Duncan had slid off the dragon's back as Tregore had been vaporized and had caught Rebekah as she passed out from shock. The King's army was cheering as loud as they could and were marching towards the castle gate eager for battle.

The Baron was not going to allow a small setback like this stop him taking the throne for himself. He grabbed Michael by the arm and with blood still dripping down his own arm from the wound the King had given him he took charge again.

"I left you to be killed, and it looks like I will have to do even that myself!"

From behind his back the Baron drew a dagger and in one swift move cut Michael's throat.

"NO!" shouted Robert.

"Wait," Zio put an arm on Robert's shoulder.

The Baron waited for Michael to fall to the floor dead, but instead he just stood there.

"Not again!" exclaimed Michael. "You have tried to kill me twice, but you have failed both times. You will not kill me or anyone else today," said a very calm Michael. "Dragon magic will make sure of that. My father always said that no matter what happens, however bad things seem, good will always win."

"We will see about that," Blackheart stormed. Then turning to the King he said, "You may have killed Tregore and have a dragon on your side, but the law of the land still states that unless you have the crown you shall not be king. You will never have the crown because I have stolen it and buried it in my castle foundations and not even I can get if from its hiding place!"

The Baron realized what he had said but too late.

"So that is where the crown went. I felt sure that you must have had something to do with it. As you rightly state I cannot reign without it so how do you intend to rule without a crown?" questioned the King.

"Since when have I worried about rules?" Blackheart

laughed. "For now I will withdraw my army to the woods, but I will be back this time tomorrow to accept your surrender. If you do not step down and hand the kingdom to me I will bring my army to your door and kill each and every one of you. I will kill you and your family slowly and then send your bodies to the ends of the land as a warning to the peasants not to cross me! With that the Baron made a slight move of his hand and slowly his army started to drift away.

A shiver went down Robert's back, he looked at his brothers and knew that they had felt it too.

The King ordered the portcullis to be raised, and with Zio standing guard he and Queen ran to their children. Rebekah had come round and was sitting on the ground in Duncan's arms, slowly realizing how near she had come to death. Nathaniel and Adam still sat bound and gagged facing the wrong way on the horse. Gwendolyn grabbed at her boys and pulled the gags from their mouths; her husband picked up his daughter and held her close.

A knight from the King's army stepped forward drawing his sword and threw Duncan to the floor and put his sword to the back of the servant's neck.

"Just say the word sire and I will send this scum to Hell where he belongs."

Robert charged at the knight knocking him off his feet.

"Leave him alone, he helped to save my brother and he is my friend."

The King looked at Robert.

"This man was left by his master to kill your brother, and

now you want to save him?"

"Yes, he could have killed Michael and he chose not to. Instead he dug the chains out of the wall to help him."

The King was speechless and in front of all the army announced, "Today I have learned the power of forgiveness from a child."

Turning to Duncan he said, "From this day on you shall receive a full pardon and I put you in charge of the safety of all the children in the castle."

Duncan fell to his knees.

"Thank you sire, I will never let you down, I will give my life to protect the children."

Robert knelt down next to his new friend.

"Thank you for helping."

Duncan said nothing but put his arm round Robert's shoulder.

From the distance Blackheart smiled, he might have lost the battle but the war would be his. He muttered to himself under his breath, "I will have the throne of England for myself. That whole family will be dead along with those children who have come to help, I swear it."

The Baron knew that dragon magic would last three days at most then he would have all his knights hunt Michael with dogs. He was looking forward to seeing Michael ripped into pieces by his hounds.

****

The King made a decision, without checking with the Queen.

"Double the guard round the castle, call the army into the

castle walls and get my council into the Great Hall, NOW!"
The Queen looked surprised, but she was pleased that at
long last her husband was being a true King.

Christian led the way, with the Queen on his right and his
children a few steps behind. Adam, forgetting that he was a
prince, caught the King up and without a word held his
father's hand and walked into the castle with him. All those
who saw knew that the King had changed and with him his
rule would change.

Robert, Timothy, Michael and Tobias followed the knights
as they all entered the Great Hall.

"Bring food," ordered the King and at once servants
rushed to obey. Within a short time bread and meat were
brought in and laid out on the tables. Without thinking
Timothy rushed over and started eating. No one stopped
him.

"I will not allow my children to suffer again. I hereby
announce my intention to step down from the throne of
England and go into exile to protect my family. The Baron
will come tomorrow and I will ride out to meet him and
agree to his terms."

The Great Hall became totally silent as what the King had
just announced sank into the minds of all present. Timothy
stopped mid-chew, chicken leg halfway up to his mouth.

"Hang on a minute, we can beat him."

Everyone in the room turned towards the boy. Someone
snorted. Tobias grabbed his friend's arm.

"Shh, everyone is looking at you."

Timothy pulled away and marched up and stood in front of

the King. He turned and held up his hands as a knight ran forward drawing his sword. The King looked at the small boy and noticed that he was not scared of the knight or his sword. He also held up his hand. The knight stopped and looked at the King, who nodded. The knight shrugged his shoulders and backed away.

"Let the boy speak," the King ordered.

The room fell silent. At the back of the room someone shouted, "Who does he think he is? He is just a child, and not one of us. Someone give him a clip round the ear and send him packing."

Zio sneezed and the peasant who had shouted yelped and was silent.

"I said let the boy speak."

The King gently lifted Timothy onto the throne so all could see him.

"Go ahead, tell us what you are thinking."

Timothy stood on the throne, only a few short days earlier he would have been killed for less. He cleared his throat.

"Tobias, please come here." Tobias went.

"You told me that you come from my future, so you must be able to go back to when Blackheart stole the crown and stop him from taking it. That way none of this will have happened, the King will still be the King, we will still be at home with dad, and no one will have to get killed."

Tobias went red. "Er that can't happen. I don't choose where or when I go, and now I am here I can't change that."

"If you can't go back, how about if we go forward?"

Tobias began to get cross.

"I have told you that I can't choose when to travel."

Robert suddenly realized what his younger brother was getting at, and rushed forward to join him.

"Wait, I understand what Timothy means; we got here from the future, so we can get back."

People in the Great Hall were shouting and laughing. The King was confused. He knew that the boys had got to his castle from another time but he did not understand how. He called for quiet.

"Please boys, will you explain what you are talking about."

Robert looked at his brother.

"Go ahead, you tell them, it is your idea."

Timothy took a deep breath.

"As you know we have come from the future to help the King. We came through a passage from our house and ended up in Tregore's cottage."

The crowd became uneasy at the mention of that name.

"If we go back to our time," Timothy continued, "the Baron's castle is in ruins and I am sure that we could find the crown. If we have the crown then Blackheart will never be King!"

A cheer went up from all in the room. The King sat down heavily on his throne, and knocked Timothy over who was still standing on it. The boy ended up sitting on the King's lap.

Tobias started to get excited.

"We could do it, we really could!"

The King made a decision, again.

"Right, here is my command. Tobias, you and the boys are to go and see if you can do what Timothy has suggested, but I'm not quite sure how."

Timothy looked at the King and struggled to get off his lap. "Please can we take the royal children as well, because they know what we are looking for?"

Nathaniel looked at his father.

"Please can we go Father? The more people looking the more chance of finding your crown."

King Christian, who this time was not ready to make that decision on his own, looked at his wife, who nodded.

"All right children, you may go. At least Blackheart will not be able to follow you there."

At the far end of the room Michael wiped his eyes as a tear rolled slowly down his cheek and quietly under his breath so no one heard he said, "Dad, I'm going to see my dad again."

20

The King's private chamber was noisier than it had ever been before, there were children rushing about all over the place.

Timothy was trying to find if there was any food left, Robert Michael and Tobias were talking to the royal children and telling them what the 21st century was like. The Queen was fussing about the children, as usual.

"We must make sure you will be safe. Christian, order some knights to escort the children and kill anyone that tries to stop them."

"Yes dear."

Timothy stood to his feet.

"Wait, if we have lots of people with us then we might get stopped. My dad promised to take us to see the castle at the weekend, I'm sure that he won't mind taking a few more."

Michael nodded.

"Dad always told us we needed to make new friends, but I don't think he meant from the past!"

Tobias smiled but said nothing.

Rebekah had been thinking.

"Father, I remember when you sent me to watch the boys by Tre… by the cottage in the woods, I heard them talking about the fireplace."

"That's how we came here."

Rebekah held up her hand, Timothy was quiet.

"If that is the way we have to go to the boy's world how are we going to get to the cottage when Blackheart's men are in the woods?"

"We need a diversion," began Tobias.

"No we don't!" Nathaniel jumped up. "We need a dragon!"

The King smiled, and looking up at the guard, he nodded. The guard at once opened the door and spoke to the guard in the corridor who in turn summoned a servant who ran off to fetch Zio.

Timothy looked at the Queen and smiled, she could have been the mother he had never had. He walked over to her.

"Excuse me, don't worry about your children I will look after them for you."

The Queen was taken aback; she had never been spoken to like that before. She gently rubbed Timothy's hair.

"Thank you."

There was a gentle knock at the door and Zio's head squeezed into the room.

"You called for me sire?"

"Yes Zio. You proved yourself by saving Michael's life, and now I have a new and very important job for you. Are you ready to serve your King again?"

"Sire I will serve no one else!"

Zio tried to stand smartly as he spoke but as he was much taller than the door he got his wings caught in the door frame. As he fell down his tail sent the guard standing outside crashing to the floor.

"Zio, please be careful or you will hurt someone."

"Sorry sire."

Adam walked in to the room with his bow at the ready, an arrow already on the string.

"If anyone tries to stop us I will shoot them!"

Without thinking, Adam relaxed his grip on the arrow for a second and it shot off the bow and bounced off the wall before hitting the guard on the head.

"Oww! Please Your Highness, be careful."

The Queen gently took the bow from her youngest son and put it out of reach.

"I only wanted to help you stay King, Father."

The King picked Adam up and held him close.

"And so you shall son, and so you shall."

The King turned his attention back to the dragon.

"Zio, the children need to get to Tregore's cottage in the woods, but it is surrounded by Blackheart's men. Could you come up with a diversion?"

Zio smiled.

"Sire, nothing would give me greater pleasure. I could fly low through the woods and chase them out with fire. The children could then run behind me."

Nathaniel and Adam started to jump around.

"Oh yes, that would be fun, and I could shoot anyone who doesn't run. Mother please can I have my bow back?"

"No."

The King coughed, and everyone looked at him. He beckoned his children to him. Rebekah ran and gave her father a big hug, Nathaniel and Adam did the same.

"The time has come my children, are you sure that you want to go through with this? You do not have to go if you don't want to. I can still step aside and let Blackheart become king. I am sure the King of Spain would give us shelter."

Rebekah stood back, disgusted.

"Father this is not just about you or us. This is about England! We must never let our country be taken over by such a wicked man. We must do whatever it takes to stop him."

King Christian could feel his face redden.

"Of course dear, I just don't want you to get hurt."

Rebekah took her father by the hand.

"I trust Robert and his brothers. If he says that we will be safe then I believe him." The princess turned and looked at Robert and smiled.

Robert coughed, he felt his face redden as he realized just how pretty the princess really was.

"Excuse me, but if we are to go back to our time then my brothers and I will need to be in our own clothes. These ones would look silly in our time."

The Queen took a parcel out from a cupboard and handed it to Robert.

"I agree. Here are your clothes, go and change before you leave."

The three brothers ran to the room they had been sharing with Tobias.

"The last time I was here," began Michael, "I was shaken awake with a dagger to my throat and dragged off to that horrible man's castle."

Timothy put his hand on his own magic dagger.

"I think we should take our daggers with us, just in case."

Robert thought for a while.

"All right but we must not tell dad, we don't want him to take them away from us. You both know he doesn't like us to play with things that could hurt us."

All of the boys fell about laughing, remembering all the dangerous things that had happened to them over the past few days.

"Dad would go nuts!" laughed Timothy.

Tobias again smiled to himself.

After a lot longer than was needed the boys made their way back to the King's private quarters. Their school clothes now seemed strange and uncomfortable to them. The guard at the door opened it and bowed to the children.

"Go with God young sirs."

The King, his wife, a dragon and seven children walked through the castle towards the drawbridge. As they went, all the servants lined the way and as the party passed them by they all bowed to the ground. Robert, Timothy and Michael felt embarrassed but the other children were used to it. One of the maids ran up to Rebekah and fell to her knees.

"Please take care my lady; I don't want to have to work for the Baron."

Rebekah stopped and put her hand out and helped the servant to her feet.

"Have no fear, we will return with the crown or we shall die trying."

The King and Queen looked at each other, their daughter

was a little girl no more.

As they reached the castle walls the King ordered that they stop. They both embraced all the children and wished them God's protection.

The Queen turned away trying to hide the tear in her eye. Timothy noticed it and went up to her and took her hand in his.

"We will be back, don't worry. I know my dad will take good care of us, he's great."

Gwendolyn tried to smile but could not hide the tears in her eyes.

The King turned to a guard and nodded. The drawbridge hit the ground with a crash loud enough to wake the dead. Zio pushed past the King and was first out of the castle, fire trickling from his nose. About 300 yards away some of the Baron's men looked up on hearing the noise, but seeing the dragon they decided it would be safer if they pretended that they had seen nothing. They looked down and resumed their card game.

Rebekah took charge. She ushered her parents back inside the castle.

"Mother, look after father, if we do not make it back you and father can still get away and live in Spain."

The Queen nodded and led her husband away.

"Go with God."

"We will. Zio, time to clear the way."

Zio took a deep breath and slowly started to flap his huge wings, knocking Tobias over with his right wing and Adam with his left one.

Both boys picked themselves up, Adam muttering something about wishing his mother had given him his bow and arrows back. Zio lifted off the ground and flew off flying low, only a few feet above the ground. The procession started towards the wood. A few of the Baron's men in the woods tried to stop them but soon backed away when the bushes around them were burned to the ground.

Blackheart was in his tent on the far side of the hill unaware that anyone had got out of the castle. None of his servants told him, they all knew if anyone gave the Baron bad news they would be killed. As the children neared the cottage a chill went down the princess's spine as she remembered how close she had come to being murdered by the man who had once lived in it.

One brave but foolish knight stood in the way.

"You shall not pass!"

"Oh yes we will!" Zio said and suddenly the knight was cooked in his own armor. He only screamed once.

The cottage had a light showing from one of the windows. Robert crept up to the back of the cottage and peeked in. Sitting round a roaring fire were about twenty of Blackheart's men. Robert crawled back to where his friends were hiding.

"The house is full of soldiers!"

Zio looked grim.

"Not for long."

The dragon waddled over to the cottage and poked his head through the window. The boys heard a scream and saw a blinding light. After a few seconds there was silence and darkness and a smell of burning flesh.

"Smells like one of dad's burnt barbeques!" exclaimed Timothy.

Tobias grabbed Timothy's arm as the boy tried to get to the food he thought he could smell. Timothy suddenly realized what the smell was and felt sick at the thought that he had wanted to eat. Zio came back to the hiding place.

"It is safe to go into the cottage now."

The children looked at each other, none of them asked what had happened to the soldiers, they all knew.

The cottage was quiet as the children entered. The walls were blackened from Zio's fire and some armor still smoldered in the corner as the men had tried to escape the inferno, and failed. Apart from that it looked just like the children remembered it. Pots still hung from the walls and Tregore's big bed was still in the corner covered in animal skins. Robert, Timothy and Michael looked at the door in the back of the fireplace and all their thoughts were far away from the King and the crown. Robert tried to hide his feelings. Would his father be cross? They had been away for ages. None of the boys could take their eyes off the little door. They could see the way home, but the fire in the grate prevented them from getting close.

21

While the children and Zio looked at the fire, Adam very quietly took down one of the big cooking pots hanging from the wall and went outside. After a short while, all in the cottage heard a loud clang, followed by a thud. The children rushed out followed by the dragon. There lying on the ground was a knight in full armor with a dent in his helmet, with a very happy young prince standing on the knight's back.

"What happened?" asked Nathaniel, checking his brother was not hurt.

"Well I came out to get some water to put on the fire, and this knight tried to rush me, so I hit him with a pan!"

Slowly the knight started to come round. He was roughly handled by all the children and forced to his knees. His visor was eventually lifted, as it was bent and full of dirt from where it had hit the ground when he fell.

"Oh!" said all the children.

"Yes! Oh," said a rather cross Sir Kempston Baignard.

"The King told me to come and make sure that you were safe. I have dodged my way through the woods and avoided all Blackheart's men, only to be bashed on the head when I got here!"

Adam tried to hide the pan behind his back.

"Sorry, I thought you were going to hurt me, so I hurt you first."

"Do not worry young master, what you did was right but next time please check who it is before you hit out!"

With that, and with the help of the dragon, Sir Kempston got to his feet. Tobias and Robert filled the pan with water from the stream and carried it together into the cottage. With a loud hissing the fire went out as the water was poured on to it. As the steam died away the door came once again into view. The knight had to grab Michael as he tried to rush to open it in his hurry to get to his father.

"Wait, the handle will still be hot."

He took off his battered helmet and gave it to Adam.

"Go and fill it with water and we will cool the door."

Adam was gone only a few moments and returned with the water. Tobias took it and gingerly walked over the embers of the fire and tipped the water on the door handle. There was more steam and hissing and then slowly Tobias reached out his hand and touched the handle. It was still warm but bearable! Michael ran across the fire and grabbed the door.

"Wait!"

All the boys and the dragon turned towards Rebekah. She called them all to her. She took Tobias's hand and gestured for all the others to hold hands.

"No matter what happens once we get to Robert's home we will be friends forever, do you all agree?"

All the children held their hands aloft and as one shouted, "FRIENDS FOR EVER!"

"It is time."

Robert grabbed Michael as he again rushed for the door.

"We will all go together. We all want to go home and see dad."

Timothy was the first to reach it and he pulled it open with all of his strength.

22

Blackheart was furious. He had woken at dawn ready to take over the throne of England. One of his guards had told him the royal children and the visitors had escaped. The Baron was at that moment walking up and down in his tent, waiting for the captain of the guard who had been ordered to watch the castle.

There was a gentle cough outside and a knight entered, his head held low looking at the ground.

"Master, I can only…"

"WHAT DO YOU MEAN BY LETTING THEM ESCAPE?" demanded Blackheart.

The knight knew that he was in more trouble than he had ever been before and as he spoke his foot scraped at the ground in the tent.

"Sire, we had no way of stopping them, the dragon was with them and he cleared the way with fire. Some tried to stop them but they were burnt in their own armor."

"Only what they deserved."

The Baron could not contain his fury and with one move he grabbed the sword that lay on his bed and before the captain could make a move his head was rolling across the floor. The body fell on its knees before slumping forward. At once a servant who had heard the shouting rushed in and seeing the dead knight he picked up the head and threw it out of the tent and left dragging the body out of

Blackheart's tent by the feet.

****

The tunnel was as it had been when the three small, scared boys had come down it the first time but somehow the same boys didn't seem so small now, or scared. As the children disappeared from view Kempston turned to Zio.

"Do you think we will ever see them again?"

"Let's hope so for all our sakes."

The knight and the dragon walked out into the wood.

"Come on I'll give you a lift."

Sir Kempston climbed on to Zio's back.

"Did you know St George was related to me?"

Zio snorted and started to fly home.

****

The passage started to narrow and smell musty. Nathaniel shivered, it reminded him of the tunnel that Tregore had led him down only a short time ago. Adam quietly took hold of his brother's hand, he felt scared too. Rebekah walked over to her brothers.

"We will be safe with the boys; this is the start of a great adventure!"

Timothy and Michael started to run, followed by the others. In the distance they could see a door. On the other side of it was their home and, more importantly, their father. Robert was the first to reach it. He stood in front of it.

"Get out of the way," demanded the twins together.

"Wait, we have been away ages, dad might be cross; we might get in lots of trouble. Tobias, you and the others stay here till we call you. Timothy, Michael and I will go first and try to explain to dad what has been going on."

Tobias smiled to himself, but said nothing he just nodded.

The three brothers took hold of the handle and pulled. Slowly and with a terrible amount of squeaking the door opened. Inside, the cellar was just as the boys had left it. The light was still on and the boxes were in a heap where the boys had thrown them when they had been trying to get to the door. Michael was the first up the stairs followed by his brothers. The three of them lay breathlessly on the hall floor. The house smelt as it always had. The coats were on the hooks by the front door as normal. In fact everything looked as it should.

"Is that you boys? Come and have your breakfast, it's on the table."

"DAD!"

All three boys jumped up off the floor and ran to the kitchen where their father stood making himself a cup of coffee. The boys stopped by the door, looked at each other, and then charged at their father, knocking him over. The four of them started rolling around on the kitchen floor laughing.

"Wow boys this is nice, what have I done to deserve all this? Why are you in your school clothes, have you forgotten it's Saturday?"

"We didn't mean to be away for so long but we couldn't get back, there is this King that needs our help, and we have met some new friends and Michael got killed and... and we are really sorry, please don't be cross."

Robert felt a lump rise in his throat.

"Robert, slow down son."

"Dad, it was my fault, I was the one to go down to the cellar first, not Timothy or Michael."

"Boys, boys what are you talking about? You are behaving as if you have all been away for ages. I don't know what game you are playing but it is time to stop now. Sit down have your breakfast."

Their father, Jack, sat and started to drink his coffee.

"But Dad," began Robert, "we have been away for ages. We came down and couldn't find you so we went to look for you."

"I was just in the garden, putting out the rubbish. I stopped to talk to the old lady next door, she's lost her cat."

"Oh, we didn't think of looking in the garden." Robert felt silly. "We couldn't find you so we looked in the cellar."

"In the cellar?" their father interrupted. "You know that is out of bounds don't you?"

"Yes, but we wanted breakfast so we went down and we found this door that led back to Old England."

Their father tried to take in all the news from his excited children. He had his back to the hall door and he did not see Tobias come up from the cellar and into the same room.

"Hello Jack," said Tobias.

23

Jack stood up and spun round so fast his chair skidded across the floor and hit the wall before falling over.

"Tobias!" he said scooping the boy up and giving him a bear hug. "I haven't seen you in years! How have you been?"

Robert, Timothy and Michael sat open-mouthed at the table.

Up the stairs from the cellar came Rebekah, Nathaniel and Adam. Tobias managed to get out of Jack's embrace and introduced the children.

"This is Princess Rebekah and the Princes Nathaniel and Adam. They are the children of King Christian and Queen Gwendolyn."

"Pleased to meet you." Jack held out his hand.

"Where are we?" asked Nathaniel.

"Woodbridge in Suffolk."

"I know Woodbridge, but I have never seen a home like this. What century is this?"

"The twenty-first," replied Jack.

Rebekah, Nathaniel and Adam looked at each other. They all had turned pale.

"Oh."

Robert had stood up and run to Jack while he had been talking. He hung onto his father's arm.

"DAD, how do you know Tobias?" Robert interrupted his

father and asked what he and his brothers were all thinking. Their father led the way into the lounge.

"It is a very long story. I first met Tobias when I was twelve. I found a small door in the wall of your grandfather's attic I opened it and fell into London in 1605. I met Tobias and we heard people talking about blowing up the Houses of Parliament. We thought we had managed to stop that, then a man called Thomas Percy managed to hire a cellar under the House of Lords. Tobias and I were able to bring the guards to the cellar on the 4th of November so no one got hurt."

Timothy looked at his father.

"Do you mean that we have fireworks on November the 5th because of you and Tobias?"

Jack looked at Tobias who just smiled.

"Well I suppose so, but there was much more going on than just us."

Adam was getting bored with the history lesson; he had been looking round the room.

"What is that?" he asked, pointing. Timothy smiled and winked at his brothers. He picked up the remote control and turned on the TV. Rebekah, Nathaniel and Adam were transfixed.

"What is it?" they all said.

For the next hour Timothy and Michael had great fun showing their visitors from the past all the advantages of living in the twenty-first century. Adam was, however, upset to find out that there were no more knights riding around on horseback. But the games console made up for it.

Robert and his father sat with Tobias in the dining room making plans. The castle where the Baron lived in 1384 was now open to the public and could be visited. Jack picked up the local paper and placed it on the table open to the center pages. There was a big photograph of the Baron's castle under the heading:

'Castle dig. Archeologists looking for 14th century crown.'

Tobias looked at Robert.

"We have to act now! If someone else finds the crown the whole of history will have been changed."

"Right, that settles it then," Jack said, getting up from his chair. "We must leave at once I'll get the car."

"What's a car?" asked Nathaniel, sticking his head round the door.

Timothy ran into the room having just been beaten at his favorite TV game, again.

"Dad, don't you think we ought to get some food? I'm hungry."

"You're always hungry," laughed his father. "We will eat on the way".

Timothy ran into the lounge to get the others. Robert was dispatched to find some clothes that the visiting boys could put on.

As Robert came downstairs with some clothes for their guests he heard a funny noise coming from the cellar. It sounded like a small cat was trying to get into the house.

Timothy made a move to open the door but his father stopped him.

"Wait we do not know who it is, it could be the Baron or one of his soldiers."

Robert stepped in front of his father and slid the bolt across the door, locking whoever or whatever it was in the cellar.

"Well done son, I should have thought of that."

"Shh, listen," Michael put his finger to his lips.

Everyone turned towards him. Michael had got as close as he dared to the door and was trying to listen.

"Someone is speaking."

Nathaniel looked at his sister.

"I wonder, do you think…?"

Rebekah and Adam looked at each other.

"Well he has done it before when we sneaked him in to the castle when we were little."

"WHAT?" shouted Robert, Timothy and Michael together.

Nathaniel waved his hand and went and put his ear to the door, as did everyone else. From the other side they heard, "Hurry up and open the door I am getting cold."

"It is him!!" exclaimed Nathaniel, as he grabbed the bolt and slid it back. He knocked the others out of the way as he threw open the door.

As it opened all the children crowded round to see what was inside. Zio stood on the top stair; he had shrunk to about the size of a domestic dog.

"About time you opened the door, I was thinking about going home."

"Zio, I knew it was you!"

Nathaniel scooped up the dragon and held him close.

"Wow, how can he do that?" asked Robert.

"I told you that dragons are magic. Not only can they change color but they can also make themselves small or big if they need to," said Nathaniel, pleased to have his pet with him.

"Yes, we can but it is not easy. When I got back to the castle the Queen was worried that she would never see you lot again, so I was ordered to come to protect you. I tried to get through the tunnel but I got stuck so I had to make myself small. But as I am here now…"

Zio shook himself and slowly started to grow and turn yellow.

"NO!" shouted Jack "You will knock my house down!"

Zio grunted and shrunk back to his small size.

"Oh well, I suppose I will be able to hide better like this."

Robert looked at the dragon.

"How are we going to be able to get him into the castle? I know that dogs are allowed in but I don't know about dragons!"

Michael ran upstairs to return with his school bag, which he gave to Nathaniel. Zio looked at the bag and then at the prince.

"If you think that I am going to get in that…"

No one heard the end of the sentence as Nathaniel picked Zio up and put him in the bag. Michael zipped it shut and Zio could be heard muttering inside.

****

Jack led the way out to the garage where he and his sons watched the faces of their young visitors as they saw a car for the first time.

Adam stopped in his tracks.

"What is that?" he asked, pointing.

Tobias laughed. "That is a car, well a minibus really, a sort of cart but with no horse. Where I come from it is very old-fashioned. The ones in my time fly."

Jack was a bit upset by this as it was brand new and all his friends thought it was the best one in the street! Rebekah walked slowly around it touching it gingerly as she did so. Jack got in and without saying a word started the engine. The three visitors jumped back. Rebekah ran from the garage grabbing her two brothers by the hand and pulling them with her.

"It is a monster, run before it kills you!"

The three of them ran as fast as they could and hid in the bushes beside the garage. Robert, Timothy, Michael and their father laughed. Robert laughed so much that he fell on the floor holding his side. Tobias shook his head and went over to the terrified children. He reached out to Rebekah and taking her hand he picked her up. She was as white as a sheet and trembling with fear. Tobias tried not to laugh.

"Come on, it is safe; there is nothing to be frightened of."

He led the way over to the car, opened the door and got in. Rebekah looked in and very carefully touched the seat. Her two brothers peeked out from behind the bushes. Very slowly and gingerly the princess got in and sat in the back. Jack looked at her.

"No princess is going to sit in the back of my bus. As the

only lady here you must sit in the front."

With that he opened the front door for her, and made a slight bow as she got in. Rebekah smiled to herself, she suddenly felt very important. Timothy and Michael climbed in and put on their seat belts. Timothy beckoned to Nathaniel and Adam who were still hiding behind the bushes.

"Come on, it's perfectly safe. Dad is a good driver."

Adam was the first to get in. He squeezed in between his two friends. Nathaniel got in and sat beside Robert. Jack picked up the bag with Zio in that Nathaniel had dropped as he ran to hide and put it in the back of the car after checking the dragon was all right. He then backed out of the garage. After he had closed the garage doors Tobias got in. Jack turned to the children.

"Ready to go then?"

The three royal children gasped as the minibus sprang to life and Jack turned onto the road.

"There are lots of them!" Rebekah gasped.

As they drove along Robert and Tobias again told Jack everything that had happened while his sons were away. He was told about the King's problem with the Baron and how Michael had been killed and brought back to life by a dragon. Jack looked at Tobias, only half-listening to what they were saying. He was just glad to see his old friend again and to be involved with a new adventure.

24

Baron Blackheart had been busy, since he'd found out that the children had escaped. He began to lay siege to the King's castle. He had brought up a trebuchet and other siege engines. King Christian had also called on his trebuchet, the one Robert had climbed. But because the King had not felt the need to train anyone to use it the first stone that the King's men tried to throw over the castle walls had fallen short, narrowly missing the castle cook, but sadly flattening Zio's stable.

This had caused much amusement among the Baron's men who were well trained. The first stone loosed from their trebuchet had landed a huge rock through the roof of the castle's kitchen. King Christian called for Sir Kempston Baignard (who had recovered from his beating from the young Prince Adam).

"What do you think we should do? If we don't give in to the Baron's demands we may not have a castle left to defend."

As he spoke another rock crashed against the castle wall sending a judder through the whole castle.

"Sire, if we give in then you will have sent your children away for nothing. I suggest that we offer Blackheart a hostage."

"Why offer that evil man a hostage? What good will that do?"

"Sire, if we hand someone over who is respected the Baron might take time to decide what to do with him and that, in turn, would give us time to call in some help from the north."

"Good idea, then he might stop bombarding the castle as well. See who you can find who is prepared to be a hostage.

****

A little while later the Baron was disturbed when a page ran into his tent.

"Sire, a knight is coming out of the castle carrying a white flag."

The Baron smiled to himself and called his advisors to his side.

"It looks as if the old fool has seen sense at last. I am at last about to take my rightful place on the throne of England."

The advisers looked at each other and gave a cheer, as they all knew that was what the Baron expected. Blackheart strode out of the tent and at once his horse was brought to him. As he swung himself into the saddle he shouted to his followers, "Let us go forward to victory! This day a new England will arise, a land where we can be strong, a land where I rule with power and not softness!"

With that he turned his horse and rode off towards the oncoming rider.

The Baron's camp was at the top of the hill overlooking the King's castle and behind the castle Blackheart could see the sea shimmering in the sun. He smiled to himself as he rode along; he knew that there would be terrible bloodshed over the next few weeks. The royal family would have to be put to death along with all their followers. Blackheart knew that in time he would have all the peasants groveling at his feet. After England, the Baron decided that he would take France and then move through the rest of Europe and he would become more powerful than the Roman Emperors of old! He laughed to himself as he rode; the man was power mad.

****

King Christian, his wife and Sir Kempston stood on the battlements of the castle and waited. The King could only imagine what was going through Blackheart's mind. Nothing good, the King knew that. The Baron stopped a few hundred yards short of the castle. He knew that at this distance even the King's best archer could not reach him. The King knew it as well, and descended the stairs to the courtyard.

There was a low rumble and the drawbridge crashed to the ground and fifty of the King's personal bodyguard galloped out with their King as he rode out to speak with Blackheart. They would protect him with their lives if necessary. The King was mounted on a white horse and his armor shone in the sunlight. No one noticed that he was holding very tightly to the saddle to ensure that he stayed upright on the horse. No one was going to see him fall off and make a fool of himself.

Sir Kempston Baignard joined the King's party as they galloped across the open ground to meet up with the knight with the white flag. Together the continued until the two enemies met halfway between the Baron's camp and the castle. Blackheart was the first to speak.

"So, where have you sent the royal children? Spain I suppose. Not that it matters for when I am King I will order their return and then I will have them publicly executed, and I will make sure that it will not be a quick death!"

Sir Kempston looked the Baron straight in the eye, his steely blue eyes looking deep into Blackheart's soul. He turned and looked at the King, who nodded. The knight turned back to the Baron.

"The rightful King of England has decided to offer you a hostage to safeguard the future of all who live and work in the castle."

The Baron snorted. "Why would I need a hostage?"

"The King wishes to ask you to give safe passage to the women and children."

"Who is to be the hostage?"

"Me."

"In that case I accept. You will be taken to my castle where you will be held without food or water until the King hands over the kingdom to me or is killed, whichever comes sooner. Everyone else who lives in the castle will not be harmed, as long as they swear allegiance to me."

With a wave of his hand the Baron summoned one of his knights who bound the hands of Kempston and led him away.

The King turned to the Baron.

"I am not dead yet," and with that he turned his horse and galloped back to the safety of his castle.

25

Nathaniel and Adam watched open-mouthed as cars whizzed past them and every time a car went past Rebekah hid her face in her hands and let out a small shriek. Robert, Timothy, Michael and Tobias sat chatting as normal.

"Dad."

"Yes, Timothy?"

"I'm hungry."

Jack laughed. "Okay, we'll go through the drive-thru and get a burger and chips."

"And a Coke?"

Jack laughed. "Okay son, and a Coke."

"What is a burger?" asked Adam

After a few more minutes the car turned into the fast food restaurant and Jack opened his window and spoke into a small box on a stand. Nathaniel and Adam looked at each other and Adam shrugged his shoulders.

"Please drive to window two, your order is ready."

Rebekah turned to her brothers.

"The box talked!"

Robert and his brothers could not hold the giggles in any longer and laughed out loud. Jack drove round to window two and, after paying the lady behind the glass, he handed a bag and a drink to everyone.

Adam looked at the straw sticking out of the top of his drink.

"What do I do with this?"

"Stick it in your mouth and suck."

Adam stuck the straw in his mouth and sucked for a while, then coughed. Then let out the biggest burp that anyone had ever heard. Robert laughed so much that his own fizzy drink came down his nose. All the boys were laughing and burping. Rebekah turned to Jack and shook her head and gently bit into her burger. A jet of ketchup squirted out and hit the windscreen. Jack drove on wondering why he had not just got some crisps.

After what seemed to Michael like a long time (but was in fact only about half an hour) Jack pointed out of the window.

"Look."

The children saw the Baron's castle for the first time in six hundred years. It was now a lot different from when they last saw it.

Nathaniel said what they were all thinking, "Good, I am glad that it is in ruins. It must mean that we find dad's crown and he will still be the King."

Jack turned the minibus into the car park and stopped.

"Children, remember that a lot has changed since you were last here and now anyone can visit and look round."

From the back of the car came a muffled noise.

"Zio!"

Nathaniel and Adam rushed to let him out of Michael's school bag. Zio stretched as he was released and a small flame shot out of his nose and engulfed the bag in flames.

"I am not going back in that, it smells of old socks."

Michael looked at where his bag had once been. "Well, it was the bag for my sports kit."

Nathaniel was worried that someone might have seen the fire, but no one had.

"How are we going to get him in to the castle?"

Jack pointed to a sign at the entrance which read: 'Dogs are allowed on a lead'. He rummaged around in the back of the minibus and found what he was looking for. Jack triumphantly held up a dog's lead. Robert suddenly looked at the ground remembering his dog Rex that had died the year before.

"I thought you had thrown that away."

His father knelt down in front of his eldest son and put his arm on his shoulder.

"I think Rex would like his old lead to go to someone who has saved Michael's life, don't you?"

Robert looked away and all he could manage to say was a quiet, "Yes."

Zio looked at the lead and realized that he was expected to have it round his neck. Smoke started to trickle from his nostrils and he started to turn red as he got angry. Nathaniel looked down at him.

"You have to put it on and look like a dog so we all look like everyone else here or we will have to find another bag for you!"

Zio muttered something about it not being fair but allowed Jack to fasten the lead around his neck. The dragon looked around the car park and tried to look like a dog. He saw a poster of a cartoon dog so he turned himself pink like the one in the picture. This made Robert laugh and he stroked Zio's head.

"Could you turn brown like my old dog Rex? It would remind me of him".

Zio nodded and slowly changed color. Robert looked away remembering his pet and playing in the garden in the summer. Jack noticed his son and put his arm on Robert's shoulder together they walked to the turnstile and Jack went to pay.

"One adult and seven children please."

The lady at the counter looked at him.

"Do you want a guide book as well, it's only another £4?"

"Oh yes, I think that would be a good idea."

"That's £40 then please."

Rebekah looked stunned. "How much? My father doesn't pay his Sir Baignard that much in a year."

"Well dear, your father is an old skinflint."

Jack paid the £40 and led the children away before one of the royal children said something that would be hard to explain.

The woman stuck her head out of the window and called after them, "That's a funny looking dog, what sort is it?"

Adam turned and shouted back, "He's not a dog, he's a dragon."

Jack turned to tell her that it was a game that they were playing but he needn't have worried, he saw her talking to the next customer, tapping her head and shaking it from side to side.

26

Sir Kempston Baignard was led to the trebuchet where he was forced to kneel and wait for the Baron. He did not have long to wait. The Baron rode up and looked down on the hapless knight.

"Did that fool of a King think that I would allow anyone to walk away from the castle and accept a hostage? He will now see what I think of his pathetic offers. It's a pity that Tregore is not here, he would have liked to see this." With that he nodded and a large man-at-arms who had been standing behind the prisoner swung a huge two-handed claymore sword and with one blow chopped off the brave knight's head. Sir Kempston never even spoke, but he died as he had lived, for his King.

"Put the head in the trebuchet and throw it back."

The knight who had killed Sir Kempston grabbed the head and tossed it to the sappers manning the war machine. The head was loaded and after a call of, "Ware the engine!" the head was thrown back.

Blackheart walked off to his tent calling for the lords.

****

King Christian's castle was quiet. The King was in the Great Hall with some of his knights. His wife, looking out of the window, could see Blackheart's army in the distance. She could see the smoke rising from their cooking fires.

"Darling, it looks like they are loading another stone onto

the trebuchet."

The King got up from the throne and walked over to Gwendolyn. As he reached her a thwack could be heard and the arm of the trebuchet swung and the missile came hurtling towards the castle. It landed harmlessly in the courtyard. Christian walked back over to his knights, realizing, not for the first time, that the castle seemed very quiet without the children. He remembered being told how Robert had climbed the trebuchet, and how the Queen had told him not to say anything. He smiled to himself and offered a silent prayer heavenwards for their safe return.

"Sire," a servant entered the room, "forgive my intrusion but I think you need to see this." He held a basket out to the King. Christian looked in.

"The swine!"

He lifted out what was in the basket and found himself looking into the remains of Sir Kempston Baignard's face.

"He will not get away with this; we will fight to the death!"

He held up the head for his wife to see. She put her hand to her mouth and stifled a scream. She knew the face of a true friend even when it had been battered. The King turned to his servant.

"Bury the head and mark the grave so we know where to put his body when we find it."

"At once sire."

"And tell Blackheart's old servant Duncan to come and see me."

The servant nodded, turned and was gone. Duncan soon arrived and as he entered the room he bowed low.

"Thank you sire for allowing me to serve you, I will not let you down, I will even die for you if you order it."

The King, taken aback by the servant's loyalty, was for a moment speechless. However, he soon recovered himself.

"Now, now man, enough of that. I am well aware that you had to grovel to your past master, but you need grovel no more, stand tall!"

It was Duncan's turn to be speechless, but he stood up and looked the King in the eye nonetheless. King Christian put his hand on the old man's shoulder.

"I know that swine Blackheart stole your lands and castle when he attacked you and killed your wife."

Duncan walked to the window; suddenly he could see his wife Rachael and his two children playing in the courtyard. Ruth had been only ten and David had just had his eighth birthday. He remembered the day when the Baron had ridden up asking for help. Duncan had offered to give him and his few men-at-arms shelter. Then Blackheart had turned on him and killed his wife while she slept. He had then taken Duncan's son and daughter from their father and sold them into slavery. Duncan had been ordered to become a servant or the Baron would send orders and have the children murdered. No one hated Blackheart more than the man who turned back to the King, with moist eyes. Christian walked over to the old man and put his hand on his shoulder.

"I swear to you that when this is all over your lands and castle will be returned to you. But now I need you to be strong. You will have seen the basket that one of my servants was carrying."

Duncan nodded.

"That was the head of Sir Baignard, my adviser and friend. I need someone to take his place. I can think of no one better than you, would you serve your King as his adviser?"

Duncan fell to the floor and kissed the King's feet.

"Oh sire I do not deserve such a great honor, but if you wish it I will serve you to my dying breath."

"Good, then what advice do you have for me?"

"Sire, get everyone inside the castle walls and order as much food brought in as can be fetched."

King Christian nodded.

"See to it."

"At once sire."

Duncan stood, turned and left the room, stunned by his promotion.

****

Blackheart was in his tent pacing up and down. Lord Hampstead and Lord Nordelph sat watching him. The Baron turned to them.

"We will lay siege to the castle, nothing will go in or out. Anyone who gets out will be killed as will anyone trying to get in. There will be no exceptions, all will be killed including women and children. When the castle is taken all inside will be put to the sword!"

The two lords looked at their master, nodded and got up and went to do his bidding. Blackheart could never have known that the very children he was trying to kill were centuries out of his reach and they were, in fact, entering his castle.

****

As the children walked under the gateway they were amazed by how much it had changed. There was a house in the middle of the courtyard. Jack explained that long after Blackheart had died the new owner had wanted to put a poorhouse in place of the castle.

The children wandered around and the memories came flooding in to their minds. Timothy saw the passage from which they had carried Michael's dead body He looked at his brother and put his arm round his shoulder. Michael looked at his father.

"Dad, there is one place that I need to go."

"Oh yes, I think they are over there."

Jack pointed to a sign with the word 'Toilets' on it.

"No Dad! I mean the dungeon."

Timothy and Robert looked at each other; their father really was getting old and forgetful. Jack felt himself blush, he hoped that the children had not seen.

Tobias looked at his young friend.

"Do you really want to see it?"

"Yes, but I don't know the way because when I was dragged there it was dark and I had a sack over my head."

"I remember the way, come with me."

Tobias led them through the castle along a long corridor, and down some stone stairs. Rebekah and her brothers were chatting and had decided that their father's castle was much better than this one. Zio was pulling at his lead and hating it so he decided to grow.

"Zio!"

Nathaniel saw what his pet was doing. Zio muttered something about it wasn't fair, and shrunk back to his 'dog' size.

Suddenly they turned a corner and there in front of them was the doorway to the dungeon, Michael's dungeon. The door had long since rotted away, but one of the hinges could still be seen in the stone door frame. The roof had also fallen in and a tree was growing in the corner of the room. Ivy was growing all over the walls, but still the room made the brothers shiver. Zio looked up, the window was still there and the stump of the bars could be seen. The dragon remembered cutting them away. Michael spoke to no one but went up to one of the walls and after moving away some of the plants he found what he was looking for. Embedded in the wall were the remains of a large iron ring. And still visible were the marks on the wall where Duncan had dug some of the cement away to free him. The chain had long since gone but the small boy remembered being chained up and thinking that he would die and never see his father again. Michael looked at his father and went over to him and hugged him.

"Dad."

"Yes?"

"I love you."

Jack said nothing, he just held his son. He could not imagine the pain his son had gone through.

The royal children out of respect said nothing and waited outside the room, they knew that this was somewhere that they had no right to be. Robert looked into the corner and remembered cutting, no killing his brother. He turned and with tears in his eyes he put his hand on his brother's shoulder. No words were spoken between the two boys. Michael let go of his father and looked his older brother in the eye before hugging him. For the first time since that awful day, Robert felt at peace and forgiven. Timothy remembered holding his brother's head while he passed from this life to the next. He went over to his twin and also hugged him. Michael looked from one to the other of his brothers and in a small voice said, "It's okay now, it's over. We are home, back with dad. We are safe."

Zio had grown to almost his full size and had put his wings around the boys.

"It is not over until we find the crown and return it to King Christian and restore England to peace."

The children looked at each other and nodded then Zio shrunk back to his small size. The children knew that their adventure was far from over. Together, with their arms over each other's shoulders, they walked back up the stairs, back along the corridor and into the sunlight. Jack followed, leading a small dragon on a lead who was trying to look like a dog.

27

"WHAT DO YOU THINK YOU ARE DOING?"

A man in green trousers and a green sweatshirt stood at the entrance to the courtyard with his hands on his hips.

"I asked you what you are doing. Can't you read?" the man said, pointing to a large sign that said in big red letters: DANGER DO NOT ENTER.

Jack went up to the man.

"I am terribly sorry, we did not see it, we were in such a hurry to see the dungeon. We must have walked right past it."

The man huffed.

"Don't you read the local papers? It has been in them for weeks that we're doing an archaeological dig on this site shortly."

Timothy went up to the man and held out his hand.

"Hello, my name is Timothy. I am sorry that we went where we shouldn't have. What do you hope to find when you dig? I am very interested in history."

The man looked at the small boy in front of him, smiled and held out his hand.

"My name is Patrick, Patrick Summer. I am the site manager for the archaeological exploration at this castle. You mustn't start poking around the castle you might get hurt. I know it is very interesting, but we start the dig this afternoon and it won't be safe. It's a good thing the lead archaeologist didn't catch you, he is a very grumpy man and snaps at everyone."

"Yes but what do you hope to find?"

"Well there is talk of an old crown, but it's probably just an old tale. I think we might find some old coins, bits of pottery and a few other things if we are lucky. Probably nothing of value."

Rebekah went up to Jack.

"Can we look round the rest of the castle please? You did promise."

"All right, come on, but remember, no running off. We have to stay together, I don't want any of you getting lost."

Jack might as well have been talking to the wind, the children ran off in all directions leaving him in the middle of the courtyard.

"Oh well, I might as well get a coffee."

Patrick pointed Jack towards the café and laughed.

"Kids will be kids."

Jack nodded and wandered off to get his coffee.

****

King Christian and his wife stood hand in hand looking out of the Great Hall window as Baron Blackheart steadily brought more and more soldiers within striking distance of the castle. Those loyal to the Baron had rallied round and found many men who were greedy for power. Once they had helped to remove the King they hoped that Blackheart would give them more lands and power. Gwendolyn turned to her husband and squeezed his hand tightly.

"I think we may not live to see the end of this battle. I pray that the children are safe in their new home."

Christian turned to his wife and held her close.

"If we are to die, then we will die knowing that Blackheart cannot ever find them, my love. They will be looked after. I trust Robert and his brothers; if they are together then they will be safe. Besides, Zio is with them."

****

Rebekah was leading the boys along one of the battlements while Jack was sitting under a sunshade enjoying a quiet cup of coffee. Suddenly there was the most awful scream. The sort of scream that you might make if you saw a fire-breathing dragon for the first time, especially if you didn't believe in them. The children looked at each other.

"Zio!" Nathaniel exclaimed.

Jack spluttered into his coffee.

The dragon had had enough of waiting for the children to come back and get him so he slipped out of the lead that Jack was holding and wandered off. As he walked round the corner a fly went up his nose and he sneezed just as an elderly lady was walking past. Unfortunately for the lady the bag she was carrying had burst into flames.

The children arrived at the same time as Jack. Patrick Summer was next to get there.

"What is the matter madam?"

"This dog just set fire to my shopping!"

Jack picked up Zio. Nathaniel held out his hands to take his pet and Jack handed him over.

"What have I told you about letting the dog run free?"

The boy caught on to Jack's wink.

"Sorry, Dad. I wasn't thinking, it won't happen again."

"If you don't keep him with you we will have to all go home. Now run along and play, all of you," said Jack.

Turning to the lady he said, "Madam, I am sorry that our dog scared you, but I don't see how he could have set fire to your bag."

Patrick picked up what was left of the lady's shopping and looked inside. The bag contained the charred remains of some toys she had bought for her grandchildren from the castle gift shop, a packet of cigarettes and a twisted, melted lighter.

"It looks like your lighter malfunctioned, it is a good thing you weren't hurt. If you come with me you can have a sit down and I'll get you a nice cup of tea." And Patrick gently led the lady to the coffee shop.

Jack stood wondering what he would have said if the lighter hadn't been in lady's bag. He laughed to himself, he had always told the boys that smoking was hazardous to health! Jack walked into the courtyard where the children were playing together. Rebekah was having a wonderful time running about with the boys. She was not allowed to play at home as she was the oldest and her parents always told her that she had to set an example. Zio was rushing around trying to be a dog. He tried to bark but the sound came out like a frog croaking. Jack decided to gather the children together before someone started asking questions about Zio which would be difficult to answer.

"Come on children, we must be going. It will be teatime by the time we get home."

"Coming Dad," answered Timothy.

28

Jack went to wake the children; Tobias was asleep on Robert's floor. Rebekah had the spare bed in the office and Nathaniel and Adam were sleeping in the twin's room. Jack almost fell over Adam who was sleeping across the doorway. Michael looked out of his bedroom window at the street below, suddenly he realized how light it all looked because of the street lights. He remembered looking out from the castle at night and only being able to see the yellow glow from the guards' fires just outside the castle walls or the light from the moon. He looked at his bedside clock, it read 01:00. Nathaniel and Adam were soon looking outside too, amazed at what they saw.

"Where are your guards?" asked Adam.

Adam asked again but Michael had fallen back to sleep.

Jack popped his head around the door. "Come on boys, up and at 'em. We need to leave for the castle in a few minutes. I'll go and make us some hot chocolate before we leave, and I have made some sandwiches to take with us."

"What is chocolate?" asked Nathaniel.

His two friends looked at each other and shook their heads. It was still the middle of the night, they led the way to the kitchen. The others were already there having their drinks. Jack went out to get the minibus. As he returned Adam was wiping his mouth on a kitchen towel.

"Wow! That was great! Can I have some more?"

"Another time, come on we have lots to do," Jack replied, as he threw the towel into the washing machine for later.
He led the way out into the chill air of the night and locked the door behind him.

****

Framlingham Castle was in darkness, Zio had seen to that. He had left the house before Jack and the children and flown straight to the castle and had gone round the floodlights one by one and fused the wires to each of them with a short blast of fire. He was flying up to the top of the only remaining tower trying to remember what Jack had told him to look for. He had never even heard of a burglar alarm before, let alone seen one!
In the car park Jack sat in his minibus with the children, he looked at his watch, it was 2:15 in the morning but he was as wide awake as he had ever been. Suddenly from high above he saw the blue flash he had been waiting for.
"Come on children, time to go, Zio's knocked all the lights out and has found the alarm. Robert, don't forget to bring that box."
Robert nodded and went round to the back doors and called for Tobias to help him.
Earlier in the day, as they had been planning to break into the castle, Jack had gone out to his garage and after a lot of moving old boxes about he was heard to say, "Got it!"
He would tell no one what it was that he had got. He had simply put the long box in the back of the minibus with strict instructions that no one was to touch it.
Very carefully and as quietly as possible the children got

out of the minibus and closed the doors. Rebekah shivered, she was not sure if it was from the cold or from the knowledge of what they were about to do. An owl hooted and flew low overhead, so low that Adam jumped and let out a yelp. Timothy put his hand over the young prince's mouth.

"Shh!"

Adam gulped and nodded, Timothy lowered his hand. As they walked from the car park every step was an unbearably loud crunch. Walking on tiptoes made no difference. Jack was sure that gravel sounded louder at night than during the day. They walked past the booth where only a few hours before they had confused the lady selling the tickets. Jack touched his jacket pocket; he still had the guide book. Zio met them by the great oak door as arranged. He was now about the size of a small horse, still a lot smaller than his normal size. Jack patted him on the shoulder.

"Okay Zio, time to do your stuff again."

The dragon positioned his face as close as he could to the lock and blew. A small blue flame shot out of his nose and into the lock. The boys looked at each other; they remembered that the last time they had seen Zio do that was 700 years ago at the other side of the castle when they had rescued Michael. Zio made short work of the lock, there was a small click and the door swung open. Seven children, one grown-up and a dragon peered inside. Jack flicked the switch on his torch and handed it to Rebekah who shone the light around. The castle looked bigger in the darkness and the shadows caused by the torch were scary.

Timothy took hold of his father's left hand and Adam held on to the right one. Jack led the way to the entrance of the courtyard. It looked a lot different than when they had been there earlier in the day. Now there was a digger and lots of smaller tools as well as a large wooden shed. Through the shed window they could see shovels and trowels along one wall. Down the middle of the shed was a long table with old maps on it.

"They must have started the dig," said Tobias, "or be just about to; remember what that man said when we came out of the dungeon."

Jack looked at the children.

"Okay, where do you think we should start? We might not have as much time as we thought. We will have to try to find the crown tonight."

Rebekah looked around the ruins of Baron Blackheart's castle.

"Well if I was going to hide anything important I would want it close to me. I think we should start where the Great Hall once was."

"Okay then, let's go. Robert, have you got that box?"

"Yes Dad."

"Good, come on then."

Silently, the group made their way across the courtyard to where they all agreed the Great Hall must have once stood. All that was left now was the outside wall and fireplace. All the other walls and the ceiling had been gone for hundreds of years.

"Robert, open the box, and take out what's inside."

Robert and Tobias tore the tape off the top of the box and turned the box upside down. Nathaniel and Adam looked at the strange contraption which had slid out. Rebekah was too busy watching what she thought must be bats; she hated bats.

"What is it?" asked Nathaniel.

"That, boys, is the best metal detector money can buy, or at least it was when I got it five years ago."

Jack organized the children. Robert, Rebekah and Tobias were each given a small trowel to dig wherever the metal detector indicated. The others were to stand in lines so Jack could ensure that the whole of the Great Hall floor was checked.

Jack put some earphones on his head, held the detector in his hand and started to walk towards Adam. After going only a few yards he held up his hand.

"Wow! That was fast, have we found the crown?"

All the children crowded round Tobias as he started to dig. Over their heads peered Zio. Nathaniel could feel the top of his head getting hot.

"Zio! Will you stop breathing on my head, you will set me on fire!"

"Oh, sorry."

Zio tried to hold his breath while he watched but he had to turn his head away when he needed to cough. A small patch of ground was scorched.

Tobias kept digging, and after a short time he triumphantly held up a battered and rusty tin can.

"Oh well, never mind. Keep looking Jack."

Jack started to walk back across the ground listening to the beep, beep, beep of the metal detector. The children followed waiting for him to stop, move the machine back and forth over a small area of ground but shake his head and move on again. Rebekah and the boys were beginning to lose interest with walking up and down the courtyard. Several times Jack waved at one of them to dig in a certain spot, but each time they found nothing of interest. Another drinks can, a nail, or an old coin but nothing that looked like a crown.

"Dad."

"Yes Timothy?"

"I'm hungry."

Tobias laughed. "You're always hungry, here have my sandwich."

The boy threw his cheese sandwich at Timothy. It landed in the dirt, but it was eaten nonetheless.

After they had all walked across every inch of the courtyard and found nothing Michael had an idea.

"Dad."

"Don't tell me you're hungry as well; I think Timothy has eaten all the food!"

"It's not that, but I was just thinking, if I was hiding something that I had stolen and didn't want anyone to find, I wouldn't put it where everyone would look."

"What do you mean, Michael?"

"Well, we all thought that it would be in the Great Hall, but it wasn't. I think we should look where we don't think it will be, and then we might find it."

Tobias stopped digging and came over to Michael.

"You might be right, where do you think we should look?"

"Well, I think the safest place to hide it would be in the dungeon."

Jack looked at the children.

"What do you all think?"

Rebekah thought about it and agreed, so did all the others.

"Okay then, lead on Tobias."

The corridor to the dungeon was now blocked. There had only been a sign there during the day but now, however, there was a large metal fence with a chain and padlock round it.

Jack looked at Robert.

"Go and get Zio."

The dragon, who had gone off in a huff after he had nearly set fire to Nathaniel's head, had been flying over the castle keeping watch, soon arrived.

The padlock melted away under the dragon's hot breath, and the fence was soon pulled away. Michael looked down the corridor. Tobias put his hand on his friend's shoulder.

"If you don't want to go down there I will stay up here with you while the others go down."

Michael nodded and walked back to the courtyard. Somehow it had been all right seeing the place where he died in daylight but now it was dark he couldn't handle it. Robert and Timothy also went back with Tobias and Michael. Zio followed them into the courtyard leaving only Jack and the royal children to go into the dungeon.

A light in a window at the top of the castle went out as the other children waited in the courtyard, and the shadow of a man had ducked away hoping no one had noticed. No one had.

29

From the high window a man had been watching them all, right from the beginning. He had seen Zio putting out the lights and destroying the alarm. He had watched the children dig up bits of rubbish in the courtyard. He had seen the dragon flying overhead, but he had kept quiet. He had remained hidden. He had watched as the party had gone towards the dungeon and thought that the fence would stop them. When he saw only four children walk back into the courtyard he decided to go and see what was going on. His hand gently slipped the pistol from the holster at his hip. He checked that it was loaded, it was.

Rebekah, Nathaniel, Adam and Jack could hardly recognize the dungeon from the morning. Now there were scaffold poles holding up large lamps and small pilot holes in the ground that were easy to trip up in.

Zio walked back to the entrance to the small room, he called to Jack, "Do you need me anymore? I am really tired and could do with getting some sleep for a while."

Jack looked at the children and they all shook their heads. Nathaniel went up to his dragon and put his arm around him.

"You go and get some sleep, you have helped a lot. If it wasn't for you we could not have even gotten in here."

Zio nodded and promised to check on the other children on his way to find somewhere quiet to sleep. He flew gently out of the dungeon entrance and out into the courtyard where the children were sitting on one of the benches talking quietly. Timothy had his head on his older brother's shoulder and had fallen asleep. Zio smiled to himself and slowly grew to his normal size; he was looking forward to some sleep. He knew exactly where he was going. Orford Castle was only a few miles away. He knew that the castle would not be the same as when he had last seen it but he wanted to sleep where his stable would have been. The old dragon knew that it would bring him closer to his home. He rose gently into the air and was gone.

Robert and Michael continued to talk, both finding it difficult to stay awake. No one saw the glint of the gun in the moonlight as Steve slowly and very quietly made his way to the dungeon. He could not leave any witnesses to his crime; he felt the cold steel of the pistol and knew that everyone would die.

****

Orford Castle had changed. From the air Zio could see that the old curtain walls that had once surrounded the keep in the center had long since gone and all that now remained was the keep itself. It made the old dragon sad to see how little of the castle remained. Slowly he flew round and round trying to get his bearings. After a while he eventually worked out where his stable had once stood. He landed and slowly walked around the spot where his old home would have been, a dragon tear on his cheek. Zio realized that he had not slept for days. He curled up on the ground and was asleep in moments.

****

Ten miles away at Framlingham the man saw that the children in the courtyard were asleep. He had thought about killing them first, but decided against it as the noise of the gunshot would alert those in the dungeon. He knew that he would have to kill them but that would have to wait until he had the crown. He made his way to the dungeon, cursing to himself for forgetting the silencer for his pistol. Never mind, he thought, he still had his dagger.

Rebekah had become bored watching Jack pace back and forth, sometimes stopping and then walking on again. She walked back up the passageway towards the courtyard, hoping to find the boys, instead she found the man. The princess opened her mouth to call for help but the man plunged the dagger into her throat and not a sound left her mouth. She at once fell limp at the man's feet, blood pouring from the wound; she died without a sound.

****

Gwendolyn watched as her castle was slowly destroyed by the Baron's siege engines. Both she and the King had taken shelter in the keep. The curtain walls were breached and Blackheart's men were inside the outer walls. The King took the Queen in his arms.

"I don't think we have long."

The Queen nodded, she didn't need to speak, they both knew that they would not survive the next twenty-four hours. The King looked at his wife.

"At least the children are safe, Rebekah is a sensible girl she will be able to look after her brothers in a new home. I hope that Robert's father will look after them well."

"I am sure he will dear, I am sure he will."

****

The Baron walked up and down in his tent, his advisors were with him.

"My lord, we think it is for the best if you show mercy when you take the castle. May we suggest that you order that the royal family be sent abroad to live in exile?"

Blackheart had been thinking as he paced back and forth.

"If I show mercy as you ask, the King could muster an army from Spain and return to destroy me, no mercy will be shown. All in the castle will be put to the sword!"

His advisers looked at each other and without a word they stood and walked out from the tent. They knew that their master was going to kill everyone. They would not interfere, afraid for their own lives. The Baron smiled to himself. No one would stop him, no one.

****

Nathaniel was worried.

"Where is my sister?"

"Don't worry, I expect she has found the boys and is playing in the courtyard."

Nathaniel looked at Jack and nodded. He was probably right. Both he and his younger brother had come to trust their new friend's father, he seemed to always know the right thing to do.

Adam was looking at the machine in Jack's hand and wondered if it would ever help to find his father's crown.

The man had been watching. He had heard every word that

had been spoken. He suddenly thought of the boys he had seen in the courtyard and he realized that if they came to check on the others they would find the body. Slowly and quietly he walked back up the passage. In the moonlight he found the girl's body, grabbed her by the feet and dragged her through part of the old poorhouse that had now been turned into a museum. He lifted the lid of an old chest, stuffed the body inside and closed the lid. The man knew that he would have to finish the others off tonight and be long gone with the crown before the castle opened to the public in the morning.

****

Timothy woke with a start, he was cold. He looked around. Michael was sleeping, leaning on Tobias, who was also asleep. He looked up at his older brother. Timothy smiled, he was so very lucky to have such a kind brother. He thought of some of his friends at school who were always fighting with their brothers and sisters. The small boy turned over and tried to go back to sleep. Just as his eyes were closing and he was getting used to the cold he heard his father call out excitedly from the dungeon.

"I think I've got it!"

Timothy jumped up and woke the others.

"I think dad has found it, come on!"

Down in the dungeon Jack had been walking up and down with the metal detector when suddenly the odd beep had become a constant tone. Jack had set the machine to find gold only and it might have paid off. Nathaniel and Adam had started to dig madly where Jack pointed. After a few minutes Adam had struck something hard. The three of them were on their knees now digging wildly with their hands.

Nathaniel was the first to find a large stone.

"Careful!" said Jack. "It is probably a cover for what is underneath."

Jack and the two boys dug round until they found the edges of the stone. Slowly Jack managed to prise the edge of it up with the trowel that he had been using. The boys got their small hands under and shaking, lifted it away. Behind them in the shadows the man stood watching, trying to keep his breathing steady. He was glad he was still unseen. Under the stone lay an old heavy wooden box. Jack lifted it out carefully, brushing the earth from the lid with his with shaking hands.

"I recognize that box!" exclaimed Adam. "It is the one that father keeps his crown in!"

"Then it is only right that you open it."

Jack gave the box to Nathaniel who held it out for Adam to open. Very gently the prince opened the box and took out what remained of the cloth bag that was inside. The bag had rotted over the years and something could be seen inside. Adam opened it and held aloft his father's crown.

"Yes! This is it!"

30

Timothy had been successful in waking his brothers, but it had taken time. Now the boys ran across the grass past the poorhouse and through the door that led to the dungeon. Robert thought that he heard something and stopped at the door. He grabbed Michael's arm and put his finger to his mouth. Michael stopped and looked at his older brother.

"Shh, I thought I heard something."

Michael nodded and the two boys hid in an old doorway. Timothy and Tobias ran on.

The man slipped from the shadows, gently stroking the pistol at his side. The sight of the crown had made him take a sharp intake of breath. The amber jewels in it glistened in the moonlight. He could only guess at its worth, but he knew it could make him a very rich man. A few more deaths along the way to being a millionaire would not be a problem for him.

Tobias and Timothy ran into the dungeon together.

"Oh, wow!" exclaimed the boys together.

Adam stood holding the crown above his head, a tear running down his cheek. When he spoke, the words came out as a whisper.

"Now we can return it to father and everything will be all right."

Timothy went over to his friend and held out his hand.

"Can I try it on please?"

Adam pulled the crown close to his chest.

"No one is allowed to put it on except the King of England! Not even me!"

"Sorry, I didn't know." Timothy felt himself go red in the face.

"That's all right."

Adam gently put the crown back in the tattered bag, placed it back in the box and handed it to his older brother.

"Rebekah, where are you?" Jack looked around for the princess. "Come on boys let's go and find her, she can't be far."

He started to lead the way out of the dungeon, but stopped to look at his son who had frozen looking up the passageway.

"Timothy?"

"Uuum, Daaad!"

They all looked where the boy was pointing; a figure was slowly walking down the stairs towards them, a gun in his hand.

"Who on earth are you?" demanded Jack.

"His name badge says he's called Steve, Dad. Steve…"

"Steve Blackheart."

The stranger finished his sentence for him. The children all gasped as they heard the name Blackheart.

"I believe there is a certain something you have found which belonged to an ancestor of mine. Something that you have taken from its rightful owner, me. You will give it to me and then I will kill you all, like I did the girl."

"Rebekah!" Adam called out but no one answered.

Jack made a move towards the man but Steve waved his gun at him and Jack backed off.

Steve smiled to himself contentedly.

****

Robert had been right, he had heard something. He looked at Michael and they both looked down the passage towards the dungeon. They could not see their brother but they could see the back of a man they didn't know. The boys looked at each other as they heard him say his name, sending a shiver down their spines. Robert's hand went to his pocket; he was glad that he had remembered to bring his dragon tooth dagger. He remembered what Zio had said, that it was only to be used to defend not for attack. He wondered if defending his family by attacking and hurting this man would be okay. His hand closed around the hilt of his weapon and he could feel the sweat as beads on his forehead and in the palms of his hands. He turned to his brother and saw Michael had also taken his small dagger out of his pocket and was holding it close to his chest.

"Are you ready to use it?" he asked.

Michael nodded, and saw the sweat on his brother's forehead.

****

Steve leaned on the wall, his gun aimed at Adam's head.

"Give me the crown now you fools."

Adam's hands closed round the box.

"Never, I would sooner die!"

"Fair enough."

A shot rang out and Adam dropped to the floor. Blood oozed instantly from the hole in the center of his forehead. Nathaniel rushed towards his brother but was stopped by the point of the gun. Jack, who was visibly shaken and fighting to stay together, put his hand on the young prince's shoulder.

"There is no point you sacrificing yourself as well," he said, his voice quiet but intense.

Nathaniel turned to his friend's father and buried his head into his chest and sobbed uncontrollably as his fists pounded Jack's chest.

Steve laughed wildly.

Robert and Michael slowly crept towards the dungeon.

Jack bent down, Nathaniel still sobbing in his arms, and picked up the box and tossed it to Steve.

"Here, go on, take it, if it means that much to you."

The man snatched the box and looked inside.

"Oh, it does, more than you will ever know. This crown has remained hidden for hundreds of years, and now it is going to make me very rich, richer than anyone I know. A collector is waiting for me in London. He will give me more money for this crown than you would imagine."

Tobias looked at the man with hate in his eyes.

"What are you going to do with us? You have the crown. Why not just go and leave us alone?"

The man looked at the boy in front of him.

"And leave witnesses? I don't think so."

He gently put the box down on an old window sill. The gun moved slightly in his hand and spat fire at Jack.

The gentle man died without a word, a hole through his heart. The boys cowered in the corner of the dungeon trying to get away from the weapon of death. Steve, without any hurry and with a smile on his face aimed the pistol at Timothy. Robert could hardly see for the tears in his eyes, he had just seen his father killed, but he was not going to watch his brother die the same way. He moved with lightning speed towards the killer. In one move he had pulled his arm back, but he could not bring himself to throw the dagger. He knew that it was wrong and his father had always told him to do the right thing even when it was hard to do so. Robert lowered his hand. The dagger started to jump around. The boy tried to return it to its scabbard but was unable to do so. The dagger had taken on a life of its own.

It freed itself from the boy's grip and flew with the speed of an arrow into the killer's arm. He let out a scream but he managed to get a shot off before dropping the gun. The bullet stuck into the wall inches from Timothy's head. Steve clutched at his arm in pain and tried to pull the dagger out, but the tooth blade stayed in. Everyone could hear the hissing as the blade started to dissolve in his arm. Steve stumbled and, as he reached out desperately for the crown, he could feel a numbness crawling down his arm and into his fingertips. His vision became blurred and he could feel himself becoming hotter and hotter. He pushed past the two brothers at the foot of the stairs and struggled up them into the courtyard and across to some bushes by the old poorhouse where he had hidden an old motorbike.

31

Zio woke with a start, he suddenly sensed that something was wrong. When a dragon tooth dagger is used the nearest dragon to it feels a pain in its mouth to alert it to the danger. Zio had that pain. At once he knew that the children needed him, and they needed him now. The great bulk of the dragon heaved himself off the ground and shook to wake up. As he did so his tail caught the small shed used as a ticket office when the castle was open to the public. The shed went crashing across the grass and ended up upside down in the car park. Tickets and guide books strewn everywhere.

"Oops," muttered the dragon.

He stretched out his huge wings and took off; he flew once round the castle before heading off to Framlingham.

****

Robert held onto his father's arm, now quiet and shaking, as if he were cold but he was not. Nathaniel held his brother's hand tightly, and called for his sister but she didn't come, no one came. Tobias and Michael stood together not knowing at all what to do. They had all come to know that Jack would look after them and make decisions for them, but Tobias looked at the man who was never going to help them again. He saw his friend holding his dead father tight not worrying about the blood from his father's chest staining his clothes. Tobias knew that he was the oldest now and he was going to have to take charge, but he didn't know what to do.

****

The killer had found his old motorbike and finally got it started. As he sped through the gates of the castle he could feel his arm getting colder and heavier. As he rode through Framlingham a lone dog barked as the bike hurtled past it. The dog sniffed the air after the motorcycle has passed and went back to his kennel, back to dreaming about chasing cats.

Steve knew the surviving children would recognize him. He thought about having to hide from the police for the rest of his life. He was glad he had friends abroad who would hide him for a share of the money he was going to make from selling the crown. He had to get to London, and fast. The numbness in his arm had spread to his shoulder. It frightened him. He would use some of the money to hide, but he would still be incredibly rich. Steve smiled to himself as he rode on, all was not lost.

****

Zio had seen the motorbike as he flew to the castle but as he did not know that Steve even existed he had done nothing, except nearly fly into a church spire while he was watching the motorbike rush along the road below.

****

Tobias suddenly knew what he needed to do.

"Boys, we must leave this place! Come on. Let's go up to the courtyard while I try to work out how to get away from here."

Robert was still shaking and looked as white as a sheet. He looked at his friend and nodded. Robert, glad that he did not need to take charge, led the way up and out of the dungeon. A slow and tearful procession of children made its way to the courtyard. Robert leading, Tobias, Timothy, Michael and Nathaniel behind. All Nathaniel could see as he walked was his brothers' lifeless face. The boy tried to shake the image from his mind, but it would not go.

None of the boys saw Zio as he flew down towards them but they all knew when he arrived. There was a large thump as he landed. He hadn't really been concentrating on his landing. Something about the motorcycle he had seen had bothered him. As he landed his tail had smashed through one of the picnic tables that were left out for visitors to the castle to sit at. Nathaniel threw himself at his dragon and burst into tears.

"He killed him," he sobbed. "Adam is dead. And I don't know where Rebekah is."

"What do you mean, Adam is dead? Don't say such terrible things."

Robert thought of his dead father in the dungeon below. He walked away without speaking. He walked over to one of the walls and punched it over and over again until his hand started to bleed, not caring how much it hurt. He could hardly see the wall because of the tears. He could hear Nathaniel trying to explain to Zio what had happened but all Robert could see was his father's face in his mind. "Daddy," he whispered to himself. No one heard.

****

Steve raced on through the night. Framlingham was now far behind him and he was heading towards London as fast as he could. The crown was strapped to the back of his bike. He had phoned ahead and arranged for the crown to be sold in the morning. He hoped to be on a plane to Argentina before nightfall. Steve smiled to himself, he was looking forward to a life of luxury.

****

Zio now had been told everything and the dragon was enraged. He took charge.

"Boys, come here. Now!"

The boys came. Robert still had blood dripping from his knuckles from punching the wall and the tears had made lines in the dirt on his face. Nathaniel was still standing close to Zio. He felt safer near the dragon. Michael was standing with Tobias and Timothy, the shock of their father's murder had not yet sunk in, they felt nothing at all.

"Boys, do you remember what happened when Michael died? How good will always overcome evil?"

Robert answered for the others.

"Yes."

"Well this is not going to be easy, but get the bodies, and we need to find Rebekah, even if she is dead."

The boys moved to obey. Robert wanted to be the one to get his father but he needed help.

"Tobias will you...?"

Tobias nodded and without a word went to help his friend. Nathaniel fetched the body of his brother. Adam was light and hung limply in his brother's arms. Nathaniel tried not to look at the body but kept looking into the lifeless eyes. The boy stumbled twice as he made his way to the dragon but he kept on going. He hoped that Zio could bring him back to life like he had done with Michael. Michael and Timothy wandered off, still trying to work out if they really had seen their father shot. It was the twins who found the body of the young princess. Michael stopped to rest and lent against an old chest and felt the lid move. He got up and looked inside. Both boys let out a muffled cry and tipped the chest over. Rebekah fell out. They said nothing but just took a leg each and pulled her to the dragon.

Soon all the boys arrived with the bodies. Zio looked at them; he knew that this night these boys had experienced something that would change them forever.

"Do you believe in miracles?" he said.

The boys didn't know what they believed in any more.

Zio Looked at the sky and let out the greatest roar of all time. The ground shook and a great light split the night sky.

32

Zio knew what he would have to do, he hoped the children would understand. The dragon's roar had opened a window in the night sky and a great shaft of light descended from the clouds. The children looked at the base of the light and they were sure that they could see someone standing in the light.

Tobias walked forward, as did Zio. Robert, Nathaniel and the twins were afraid and stood back. The dragon walked into the light and spoke in quiet tones to the person who was there. Tobias waited until Zio had finished, then he approached and also spoke to the being.

The person spoke out of the light and beckoned to the boys.

"Approach."

The boys walked slowly forward, still afraid.

"Come, you have nothing to fear."

The boys looked at each other. Robert shrugged his shoulders and strode forward, towards the light. The others followed close behind. They stopped about ten feet from the base of the light. Although it was the middle of the night the courtyard was lit as if it was a sunny day. Robert shielded his eyes and tried to look at the figure in the light. It had human form but Robert could see through the figure's body, it was almost transparent, like looking through water in a glass. Tobias came over to his friend and put his hand on Robert's shoulder.

"Don't be afraid, she is a friend."

Tobias gently led his friend forward.

The figure held out her hand and gently touched Robert on the other shoulder. At once the boy felt a deep peace flow through his whole body from the top of his head to the soles of his feet. He knew that everything would be all right. Michael, Timothy and Nathaniel walked forward and the lady gently touched each of them in turn. A peace washed over the boys and they became still. Zio was standing beside Tobias, his head bowed.

The lady spoke.

"Children, my name is Obney, I am the keeper of time. Zio called to me with his roar. Only in times of great need can a dragon cry out to me for help. He has explained to me what has happened to Jack, Rebekah and Adam. I have checked and the time is not right for these people to die. Zio, before you do what you know you must you have one other job to do that only you can. Are you ready to face your destiny?"

The dragon bowed low to the ground.

"I am."

Michael thought that he saw a tear in the dragon's eye but he could not be sure.

Obney spoke to the dragon.

"You must find the man who has stolen the crown and return it to me. You must take one of the children with you."

"I'll come." Tobias went to his old friend. The boy knew

what lay ahead for the dragon.

"No, Tobias you will not go. You will stay here and look after the bodies for me."

The child bowed and without a word stepped back.

"Michael you will go. You have experienced dragon power and you will be able to help."

Michael did not want to leave his father's body, but he knew he had no choice. He walked to the dragon without a word.

"Climb up on my back and we will go. Your father's body will be safe."

"Will I ever see my father again?"

"Yes son, you will but it will be at a great cost."

Michael did not understand what Zio meant. Tobias did, and he looked away. He could not face his friend as he knew what was to happen.

Zio and Michael rose into the air, the great dragon circled the castle once to get his bearings and with one look down they were gone. Tobias and Obney were left with the other boys and the three bodies. Tobias could not face the great lady but just looked up into the night sky trying to see Zio as he flew away. But he couldn't because of the glare from the light shaft shining down from the sky.

****

Zio flew towards London. Michael had heard the motorbike start as Steve Blackheart had left the castle and was telling the dragon what they were looking for. But he had had great difficulty explaining what a motorbike was. Zio was sure he had seen something like a motorbike on the way to the castle. Maybe even the one they were looking for. If only he had known, he thought to himself. The sun was beginning to come up as the dragon and the boy flew on.

Far below Steve hurtled on, not knowing he was being followed.

"There!" shouted Michael into Zio's ear. The two plummeted towards the rider on the bike. As they got closer they realized that it was not Steve.

"Sorry," Michael shouted, as the man on his way to work nearly fell of his bike. They flew on.

****

Back at the castle Robert stood looking at his father, the hole looked bigger now than it had when he was shot. Robert tried to remember the good times they had had together. For a moment he remembered playing on the beach with his brothers and their father. For the first time Robert realized that he was an orphan; he would need to look after his brothers. He wondered if maybe the King and Queen would adopt them, he was not sure if he was ready to be a grown-up and have responsibilities.

Nathaniel sat with the body of his brother draped across his lap, the back of Adam's head was partly gone. Timothy was walking around the courtyard still unable to come to terms with his father's death.

"Children, please come here."

The boys were still unsure who or what the timekeeper was and whether she was a friend or not. Tobias had told them that it was safe to go near her, but they still didn't trust someone they could almost see right through. Even so, they went over to the light as it felt strangely warm and comforting.

"Robert, do you remember how your father used to tell you that good will always win and evil never will?"

Robert looked away and nodded. His father used to say that. He could almost hear his father's voice.

"Well, your father was right, and when Zio returns all will be well. Tobias turned away, he could not face the truth. No one saw the tears, or saw the boy's shoulders shake.

33

Zio and Michael flew on. Steve rode like the wind beneath them. High above, Michael was watching him, he knew it was him, he could sense his father's murderer anywhere. The boy wanted to kill him, but in the back of his mind he could still hear his father's words, "Never allow bad thoughts to rule your life."

He tapped Zio and pointed to the speeding motorbike. Zio started to descend towards it until he was just behind the motorcycle, swooping with the curves of the road. Michael saw the rucksack with the crown inside, now strapped across the back seat. He shouted into the dragon's ear. Zio nodded and a slow smile spread across the dragon's face.

Steve Blackheart was so involved in riding the motorcycle as fast as he could that he didn't notice the dragon come alongside. He never even looked in his mirrors; had he done so he would have seen a small boy reaching out for the bike. Michael held on to the dragon very tightly and lent out as far as he could then, with a swish of his dagger, he cut the straps which were holding the rucksack in place. It tumbled from the seat onto the road and Steve raced on, not knowing he no longer had his prize. Zio landed on the road, coughed and a small bush at the roadside was engulfed in flames. Michael jumped down and opened the rucksack and took out the crown. It gleamed in the morning light. The dragon and the boy looked at each other and smiled, at last the crown was safe. Michael climbed up onto his friend's back, holding on tight to the box. Zio slowly took off and headed back to Framlingham and his destiny. The driver of the lorry that the dragon's right wing just missed thought he must have drunk too much beer the night before.

****

The light from the sky above the castle had diminished but was still there. By now the sun was up but it was still too early for the people of the town to be out of bed. The crumpled bodies still lay at Obney's feet. The boys sat quietly waiting for the return of Michael and the dragon. Robert, Nathaniel and Timothy were looking forward to seeing them. Tobias was dreading it, the timekeeper had explained to the boy what great cost the dragon would have to pay for the lives of their friends. Tobias knew there was no choice, and he hated it.

Across the sun flew Zio with Michael sitting astride him, holding the crown high for them all to see. They circled the castle and landed beside the bodies.

Obney looked at the boys. The light coming from her seemed to get a little brighter. She beckoned to them.

"Prince Nathaniel, come here."

The boy went.

The lady took the crown from Michael and handed it to the boy.

"This belongs to your father; you are to make sure that it is returned to him safely. I will watch over you until it is safe in his hands. Zio, your time has come."

Tobias could bear it no longer and he threw himself into the dragon's chest and pleaded with Obney.

"Is there no other way? Please can there be a way?"

Obney shook her head and reached out her hand and touched the boy.

"I am very sorry son but to return your friends to you there must be a sacrifice."

"WHAT!", Nathaniel shouted, rushing to his pet and hanging round his neck. Zio stood, knocking the boys to the ground.

"Children come to me."

The boys rushed the dragon, knocking him off his feet.

"Boys please sit and listen to me."

The boys sat at Zio's feet. The dragon looked at each of them in turn, with a tear in his eye.

"What I am about to do I do of my own free will. To bring one person back to life is possible for a dragon, as you all know. But to return three to life is more than I can do. I must sacrifice myself so that your family can be saved. Nathaniel, I have lived 300 years and had many owners but you have been the kindest. Remember to continue to live the way of a true prince and make your family proud of you. Tobias, we have shared many adventures and you have been a true friend. You and your new friends will continue to have many more adventures. Be at peace."

Zio looked at Obney and nodded.

"I am ready."

Nathaniel continued to hold the dragon round the neck and held on tight.

"Please don't go."

"My friend, if I don't let this happen your brother and sister will be kept from you for all time. I must do this for the future of you all. Please let me do what I have to do."

Tobias gently took hold of the young prince and led him away from Zio. He could hardly speak but he managed, "we have no choice," before he too ran to Zio one last time and hugged him.

"Be assured your death will not be in vain, I swear it."

Zio nodded and without a word folded his wings around the boy. Tobias, after wiping his nose on his sleeve, stood and looking at his friend for one last time said, "I know what you are doing is right, be at peace. We will never forget you."

Tobias managed to pull himself away from the dragon and walk back to the others. He and Nathaniel could hardly see for the tears running down their cheeks.

Obney walked over to the dragon and put her hand on him. She reached out her hand to the three bodies and looked the dragon in the eyes.

"Zio you know that only the pure in heart can do what you have offered to do, there is no one else that can do this,

I must ask you one last time do you freely lay down your life for your friends?"

Zio turned and looked at the boys, a tear in his own eye.

"I do."

As the dragon spoke he turned white, as white as new snow. The children turned away partly because they wanted to hide their tears and partly because the color was so bright.

Obney looked for one last time at Zio and smiled a deep peace washed over the whole castle and comforted the boys.

"What you do today will be remembered for all times."

There was an earth shattering roar and for a second the sky turned black as night. A single lightning bolt shot down from the sky causing a flash so bright that the boys were blinded for a split second. As the lightning died away and the sky turned back to a light blue Jack, Rebekah and Adam stood beside the charred remains of the dragon surrounded by light. Zio had given his life to save his friends, and had become a hero.

34

Jack and the children had no scars or any signs of the horrible deaths that they had all suffered. Obney held up her hand to the other children.

"Today you have all witnessed the power and love of a dragon. Never forget what you have seen this day. I now give you back your family."

Robert ran at his father, knocking him off his feet; Nathaniel ran to his sister and brother and hugged them both. The twins looked at each other before joining their brother. Tobias said nothing, he just walked over to what was left of Zio and stood watching as the remains slowly fizzed and disappeared.

"Goodbye my friend."

The boys looked around for Obney but she was nowhere to be seen. Jack managed to get everyone off of him and stood up. He was the first to speak.

"Children, we have work to do. Although we were in the next world we were allowed to see what was going on." He looked at Rebekah and Adam who both nodded.

Robert looked at his father.

"What do you mean, in the next world?"

"We were watching you from above, you have done well."

Michael looked at his father. There was a hole in the front of his shirt where the bullet had entered and when he walked round he saw that there was a bigger hole at the back. He could see his father's skin though the holes but there were no marks on it at all. He looked at Adam, there was not a mark on the boy's head either. Rebekah also looked as if nothing had happened to her.

****

Jack led the children back towards the car. Nathaniel looked back over his shoulder, all that remained of where the dragon had been was now just a patch of burned grass. Nathaniel then looked at his brother and sister. He knew that Zio really had become a hero. He had given his life for his friends. The prince looked towards the sky knowing that he would never see his friend again.

He whispered to himself with a lump in his throat, "Goodbye, I will miss you. Thank you for Rebekah and Adam and my friends' father."

Rebekah looked at her brother, and without a word went up to him and walked with him to the car. No one spoke as they drove away from Framlingham back to Woodbridge. Jack was still trying to make sense of having been shot, killed and then being returned to life. He remembered the shot then being woken in a white room by Obney. He wondered why he had felt no pain. Rebekah and Adam were thinking the same thoughts. Michael was remembering flying through the air on the back of a dragon chasing a motorbike. He smiled to himself, no one at school would ever believe him but he didn't care. His teacher was always going on at him for being a day dreamer. The others were missing a friend and wishing things had been different but knowing that they could do nothing. As Jack turned the car up the drive and parked outside the garage the sky was bright and clear and everything looked new.

The children got out of the car. They were all suddenly so tired after all that had happened. Tobias shook off the tiredness as best he could, they needed to get back to the King with the crown.

"Come on you lot we still have a lot to do."

"Not now you don't."

"But Jack…" Tobias began.

"None of you are going anywhere until you have had a few hours' sleep. All of you back to bed before you start saving your country!"

The princess looked at Jack. She wanted to go and save her family and see Blackheart beaten but she knew he was right.

"Boys, we will do as Jack says go and get some sleep."

Her brothers looked at her and without a word went upstairs followed by their sister.

Tobias looked at the twins. Timothy could hardly keep his eyes open; Michael was already halfway up to bed. Tobias and Timothy followed leaving Jack and Robert alone in the kitchen.

Robert looked at his father, seeing him in a new light.

"Dad."

"Yes."

The boy said nothing he just went over to his father and hugged him. Jack knelt down and returned the hug.

"Robert, you know I love you, now you need to know I am

very proud of you. You will find as you get older that nasty things can happen to good people, but if you continue to stay true to yourself good will always triumph."

Jack looked at his son expecting an answer. Robert said nothing. Jack smiled, his son was asleep with his head on his father's shoulder. Jack gently lifted him and took him up to his room and laid him on the bed.

Jack went back downstairs and put the kettle on, he needed a coffee. As he sat in the lounge he remembered all the adventures he had had as a boy with Tobias. He remembered years ago being told by Obney that when he became a grown-up he would no longer be able to travel through time. He would like to be able to go and help his sons restore the throne to Christian but he knew that he would not be able to. As he sat looking out of the window aware of how tired he was he drifted into a peaceful sleep. His mug of coffee dropped out of his loosening grip spilling onto the carpet.

35

Orford castle was bustling with villagers who had been brought into the castle grounds for safety. Christian and Gwendolyn were in the keep and Duncan was kept busy trying to keep the peasants' children entertained and to keep the King informed of what was going on.

Blackheart's men were now camped close to the castle. They had surrounded the castle on all sides and were following the Baron's orders to the letter. A farmer had tried to enter the castle after he had returned from the fields and two of Blackheart's men had killed him. The remaining villagers had fled to the woods; some had been lucky and got away but most had been put to the sword. Blackheart remained in his camp away from the castle. He had been furious when he'd found out the children had escaped. He would find them after he had taken the castle. The boys would be killed and when she became old enough he would take the princess as his wife. That would appease some of the peasants.

Some of his foot soldiers sat around a large fire eating venison from a spit. The Baron had ordered his army be well fed to give the men strength.

In the castle the King had ordered that everyone was to be fed as well. He and the Queen would not eat anything that the common people didn't eat.

All along the battlements stood row upon row of men,

women and children all armed to the teeth with anything that they could find. Some had swords and others had farm tools. All of them were ready to fight to the death for their King. Christian and his wife stood high up in the keep looking over their castle. They could see the damage which had been wrought by the trebuchet. The King turned to his wife.

"If by some miracle we come through this battle we must do all we can in return to help the villagers and townspeople of our land who have risked their lives to help us."

The Queen said nothing, she just was glad knowing that the children were safe with Zio.

****

Tobias was the first to wake when the alarm on his watch went off. He needed to talk to Jack while the others were still asleep. He looked out of the window, it was still light and the sun was still high in the sky. He went downstairs, careful not to wake Robert. He found Jack asleep in the armchair. Jack woke with a start at the boy's touch to the shoulder.

"What time…?"

"It's not late but we need to be off soon. You know you won't be able to come with us don't you?"

"Yes, promise me you will look after the children for me."

Tobias stood looking out of the window; he turned to his old friend.

"You also know that we will not meet again. Once we have gone back and done what we can to return the crown to the King I will be sent somewhere else in time and I will not be able to come back here with your children."

Jack stood and went to the window and put his hand on the boy's shoulder.

"I know, we have had some great adventures over the years and now it is the turn of my children."

"At least when they come home and tell you all about it you will not think they have gone mad!"

Jack laughed as he remembered trying to tell his parents about some of his adventures through time. His father had even sent him to his room once for lying.

"Come on Tobias, we must wake the others."

Tobias nodded and went to wake them; Jack went into the kitchen and prepared some sandwiches. Robert was the first one downstairs followed by all the others except Timothy. Jack called up the stairs, "Timothy, time for tea."

There was a crash as the boy fell out of his bed followed by, "Coming Dad."

Timothy came down the stairs so fast he missed the last few steps.

"Timothy! What have you done to your hair? It looks like you have stuck your fingers into a light socket."

"Sorry Dad." Timothy tried to smooth his hair down with his hands. "What's for tea?"

"What is a light socket?" Nathaniel enquired.

Rebekah then said what they had all been thinking.

"I have enjoyed being here and seeing all these new things, but we must go home to help my father."

Jack had been dreading this moment but it had now

arrived.

"Rebekah is right, you must go and be the heroes that you all are destined to be."

He handed Tobias a small bag; the boy took it and nodded to the man he had known for hundreds of years. Timothy was stuffing food in his mouth until his cheeks puffed out like a guinea pig's. Adam watched him and laughed so hard he started to cough. Robert slapped the young prince on the back.

Tobias walked over to Jack and held out his hand. Jack took it and shook it.

"Go and do what you must, keep safe and keep my children safe."

"I will do my best."

"Children it's time."

Jack led the way to the cellar door, he opened it and one by one seven children filed down the stairs. Jack stood at the top looking down.

"Robert."

"Yes Dad."

"You are the oldest of my children, I expect you to look after your brothers and to do whatever is needed to bring you all safely back home to me."

Robert looked at his father and walked back up the stairs to him.

"I will bring us all home or die trying." Rebekah opened the door to the past. Then she and her brothers looked at their new friends' father.

"Goodbye and thank you for helping us to find our father's

crown, you will never be forgotten; this I swear."

With that the girl turned and disappeared down the corridor until she was out of view. Nathaniel and Adam went up to Jack and held out their hands. Jack took hold and solemnly shook hand with the two princes. Nathaniel said, "In my castle we would never be able to do what you have let us do. You have helped us to find my father's crown. I can never repay your kindness. Thank you."

"Thank you Your Highness, go with God."

"We will."

And with that the two boys were gone.

Michael suddenly rushed up the stairs and past his father into the house.

"Where are you going?"

"Hang on Dad, I just forgot something."

He returned a few moments later stuffing something in his pocket.

Michael and his brothers looked at their father for one last time before stepping through time. The cellar was now empty except for Jack and Tobias. The boy wanted to be last as he needed to speak to Jack.

"I will keep your children safe, with my life if necessary. We have been friends for longer than anyone else in the world and although this is goodbye we will stay friends until the end of time."

Jack embraced the boy before handing him a small rucksack containing the crown. Tobias checked the straps were secure and slung the bag onto his shoulder.

"I know I can entrust my children with you, now get out of

here before they wonder where you are."

Tobias went to the old oak door, turned to Jack, waved and was gone. Jack stood at the top of the stairs looking at the open door for a few moments then went back into the kitchen and stared out of the window, offering up a silent prayer for the safe return of his children. Then he reached over and put the kettle on.

36

Inside the cottage in the woods it was quiet and dark. The only light inside it was from the moon. Rebekah was the first one to step through the door in the fireplace. She stood still and let her eyes adjust to the gloom. She looked round the room, in the corner were the remains of the armor that had contained the Baron's men. There was still a faint trace of the smell of burned flesh from when Zio had roasted the men. A shudder went through her.

Her brothers came next through the door in the fireplace. They also looked around.

"Are we really here?

The princess put her hand on her brother.

"Yes Adam."

Robert and the twins were the next to arrive followed a moment later by Tobias. The young time traveler looked at the princess.

"Princess, I have been thinking, we do not have a dragon to help us to get back to your father's castle but I think I might know a safe way into it."

Tobias beckoned to the girl and the two of them talked out of earshot of the others. Robert wanted to go and listen in to what was being said but he thought better of it. Instead he looked round the cottage. He could still remember the first time he had seen it. Was that really so long ago he wondered. So much had happened recently. He looked at his brothers, they too were walking slowly around the hut. Rebekah and Tobias returned to the center of the room.

"Boys, please come here."

The boys looked at the princess and came to her.

"Tobias has an idea and I agree that it is the only way we can get back to the castle. We will all do as he says, okay?"

Nathaniel and Adam looked at each other, they had never seen their sister like this. Normally she could be a bit bossy but this was different, she was behaving like a grown-up.

"Yes sister," they said together.

Robert looked at Tobias; he had come to trust the boy.

"Do you remember how we first met in this room?"

He nodded.

"I wanted to fight you as I thought you were horrid and rude. I was wrong then but now we will do whatever you say. My dad trusts you so I do as well."

The twins nodded.

"Good, then sit down we have work to do."

As they went to sit Nathaniel held up his hand.

"Shhhh, listen a minute."

They could all hear it now; voices were approaching the cottage.

Tobias looked around trying to find somewhere to hide. Robert was the first one to think of it.

"Quick, back into the tunnel," he whispered.

The door to the passageway shut as the last of the children disappeared from view just as the front door to the cottage opened and light streamed in as in walked Blackheart with some of his men, some of whom were carrying lanterns.

The soldiers quickly picked up the table and chair for their master and the lanterns were set up on the mantelpiece above the fireplace.

"Sire, some of the soldiers say they won't be able to bring themselves to kill all the people inside the castle. There has been talk that the King and Queen should be allowed to live. When you took over Framlingham Castle you allowed the children to live but sent them into exile in the north. Why not do the same with the peasants?"

Blackheart paced up and down in the hut, thinking. He turned to Lord Hampstead.

"The children you talk about are not in the north. I had them brought back near here in case I needed to use them to threaten the King. They are being held in Woodbridge in a barn by the river, close to the mill. Send a cart for them. We know that the traitor Duncan is now in the King's employ. Let us see how he likes watching his children burned alive. As for mercy for the peasants, none. Do you hear me? None!"

Lord Hampstead and his men looked at each other; they all knew to go against the Baron would mean certain death.

"I will send for the children as ordered sire."

"Good. Also send orders to get everyone ready. We are to storm the castle at first light. We will wait no more. The King has sealed his own and his subjects' fate."

"At once sire"

"Now get out, I must rest."

Lord Hampstead beat his chest with pride. He and the other knights backed out of the room. The Baron sat in

Tregore's huge chair, his feet up on the table, his back to the fireplace.

Robert very quietly opened the door, he had heard everything. He watched Blackheart and waited.

"Bring me ale!" the Baron shouted.

At once the entrance door to the cottage opened. Robert gulped and shut his door and hoped he hadn't been noticed. A serving wench entered the room carrying a jug and a goblet. She poured a drink for her master and left the room. The Baron drank it and threw the goblet across the room smashing it against the far wall.

Inside the tunnel the children made plans. Timothy turned to his brother in the passage.

"Robert, do you remember when we first came through this door and were given some stew?"

Robert nodded.

"Did it taste a bit funny?" said Timothy.

"Yes, I didn't eat much because I didn't like it."

Tobias looked at his friends.

"I gave Tregore a potion before you all arrived and he put it into the stew. It made you fall into a deep sleep. I think Tregore put it on the shelf above the fire. If it is still there and if there is any left we can make the Baron sleep too!"

Rebekah squeezed past the smaller boys to join Tobias and Robert by the door.

"I will try to get it."

"No princess, you must stay hidden. Robert or I will try."

The girl looked at the boys.

"And how are you going to reach it? I am the tallest of all

of us. I will get it."

The boys looked at her.

"She's right; she could reach it better than us."

Tobias shrugged his shoulders.

"Okay, then you are looking for a small brown bottle with a stopper in it. Be careful not to get any on your fingers because if you lick your fingers it will make you sleep as well."

Robert opened the door as quietly as he could. The Baron was only a few feet away, his feet still on the table. His head was beginning to nod. Rebekah looked at the boys and silently slipped into the room. She stood on her tiptoes and looked along the shelf, her hand found a small bottle and, being careful not to drop it, she took it to show the boys.

"Is this it?" she whispered to Tobias.

Tobias took the small bottle and taking the cork out sniffed the liquid. He made a horrid face and handed it back to her.

"Yes, but take care!"

Rebekah nodded and said nothing. She turned towards the Baron who now was snoring gently. His head had slipped back on the chair so that his head was facing the roof.

That makes it easy, she thought to herself.

Very slowly the girl made her way towards Blackheart. Then suddenly the door to the cottage was opened from outside the princess dived behind the Baron's chair. She could feel her heart beating in her chest and she was sure that anyone in the room would be able to hear it. The woman who had brought in the ale came bustling in.

"My lord, would you like..." She saw the man sleeping.

"Oh, sorry sire."

She backed out of the door with the jug of ale still in her hand and Rebekah composed herself, waiting for her heart to slow down.

Robert had been watching from the fireplace. He had been unable to move when the door had opened. He had stood in full view of the woman, but she had not seen him. The Baron muttered in his sleep but did not wake. Rebekah stood up carefully next to the Baron; she was shaking like a leaf as she took the stopper from the bottle. She had her back to the boys so she did not see Tobias frantically waving at her. She gently stood behind the man and slowly and deliberately poured the green liquid into the Baron's mouth. Blackheart suddenly sat up and grabbed his throat. He tried to call out but the potion had already started to take effect and all he could manage was a mumble. The princess put her hand over his mouth until he had swallowed. He did not have the strength to struggle. After a few seconds the Baron slumped back into his chair. Tobias and the other boys came out of hiding behind the door and stood looking at her.

"Wow!" whispered Robert. He suddenly saw her in a new light. She really was very beautiful.

Tobias wasn't talking, he had put his ear to the Baron's chest.

"Thank goodness!"

Rebekah looked at him questioningly.

"You only needed to use a few drops," whispered Tobias, "not the whole bottle!"

"Is he dead?" Adam asked.

"No, but I can't say how long he might sleep for. He is going to have a horrible headache when he wakes up!"

"Oh, pity," Adam said.

37

Michael was waving his hands frantically. The others noticed and were instantly silent. Robert crept with his brother to the cottage door and they listened behind the closed door. They could hear voices outside. Lots of voices. Robert gingerly opened the door bit by bit. The voices became a lot louder. He could see a large fire outside. Some of the Baron's men were drinking and talking cheerfully amongst themselves and some of the peasant women were there too, their faces flushed and glowing in the light from fire. Tobias looked over his friend's shoulder.

"Some people will do anything for a gold coin," he muttered and he carefully and quietly closed the cottage door. He called the others to him.

"Well, we won't be able to leave by the front door. I didn't think we would be able to anyway. We'll need to climb out of the back window and make our way through the woods."

He opened the shutters and looked outside, all was still. Climbing up and through he whispered, "There's no one out here, come on."

They dropped from the window one by one and crept towards the cover of the woods. Tobias waited for them all to make the cover of the trees before he took one last look at the Baron and closed the window shutters behind him and followed his friends into the woods. Tobias smiled to himself, the Baron would be in the foulest of moods when he woke up. He crept across the clearing towards the others.

"Listen carefully, I had time to have a good look around these woods when I was sent to keep an eye on Rebekah when she was playing the other day."

The princess remembered seeing his reflection in the stream the other side of the hut.

"Over there is an old path that leads to the castle moat. If we are careful and aren't seen we could be in the castle by daybreak."

"Come on then! Let's go!"

Rebekah started to walk off, the others following her.

"Princess, please take care, if we are caught we will almost certainly be put to death. Adam, it is only right that you take this."

Tobias handed the rucksack to the boy who put it on. Tobias led the way through the undergrowth to an old disused path. They were all glad that the moon was high and there were not many clouds; it made it easier to see where they were going. After they had been walking for a short time they heard a rustling sound to their left. The children froze.

"Who be that?"

No one spoke.

"I says who that be? I 'ave an arrow aimed at your 'ead, tell me who you is or I'll shoot."

Tobias stood up and signaled the others to stay hidden.

"My name is Tobias and I am here in the name of the King!"

"Oh, I'm sorry young sir. I thought you might 'ave been one of them other vermin. If you 'ad 'ave been you'd 'ave a dirty great 'ole in your 'ead now. Them scum says their goin' to kill them all in't mornin'. I feels sorry for them young uns wot came to 'elp. They ain't goin' to be no good now."

"Is that you Hendric?"

Rebekah stood up.

"Is that you Princess? Gawd be praised. Me and the missus thinks you wuz dead."

Tobias looked at Rebekah.

"You know this man?"

"Yes, he is a poacher. Father has been trying to catch him for years."

"Arr, but I is too smart for 'im, beggin' your pardon o' course your ladyship."

"Hendric, if you help us to get to the castle I will ensure that you and your whole family receive a full pardon and you and your descendants will be free to hunt in the woods for all time. Are you ready to serve your King and his family?"

The others stood up and for the first time the poacher came face to face with the royal children and their guests. The poor man fell to the ground and groveled at their feet.

"Forgive me, I am but a 'umble man I will do whatever you say, just don't 'urt me family."

"I give you my word, none of you will be harmed."

"Then you comes wiv me, I knows the way."

The old man led the children down some very narrow paths and under hedgerows and before they knew it they were at the edge of the moat. The water shimmered in the moonlight. Adam looked at the castle, he was nearly home.

"How do we get across?" he asked.

"We swim." Tobias stepped into the water and found it was colder than it looked.

"Come on, let's swim across, we can do it."

They had been seen from the fringe of the woods. A lone archer from Blackheart's army had been following them at a distance from the cottage. He gently lifted his bow and placed an arrow in it, and aimed it at the princess.

Rebekah decided that Tobias was right, the only way home would be to swim. She gently lowered herself into the water, just as the arrow embedded itself in the tree inches from her head. The archer cursed his luck and put another arrow to his bow string, determined this time to find his target. Perhaps a little lower, he thought. It was to be his last thought. An arrow struck him between his eyes and he fell silently into the undergrowth. Hendric walked back to the children shouldering his bow, he felt it best to keep to himself how close Rebekah had come to death. One at a time the children lowered themselves into the moat and started to swim across to the castle. Hendric followed close behind.

Robert was the first to reach the safety of the castle walls, but he did swim for the school team, so he expected to be first. Tobias was next followed by the rest. Hendric came in last. Rebekah looked at the old man.

"You didn't need to come, you have done enough."

"I 'ad to come, 'ow does you fink you're gonna get in to de castle wiv out me?"

Tobias looked at the walls. He led the way as quietly as he could, which was difficult as Adam was overjoyed to be so close to his home.

"Adam! Be quiet!"

"Sorry."

The young time traveler knew that somewhere around the bottom of the castle wall there was a hole where the waste from the chamber pots was thrown out. It would stink but it was the only way that he could think of getting into the castle. As the group neared the end of one of the walls Timothy looked round the corner. He could smell the hole before he could see it.

"Tobias, we can't go that way!"

"I know it smells bad but we have no choice."

"No, I mean we really can't go that way, look."

Tobias and Robert peaked around the corner of the wall. Standing a few feet in front of it was a knight in full armor with his sword drawn. Neither of the boys had noticed him before but as a cloud moved from across the moon he had become visible. The two boys shrank back along the wall. Tobias beckoned for the others to stay down and then slowly they all moved back from the corner. Rebekah spoke to the boys, she had decided that she would go round to the guard and hope that he would not kill a princess.

"Err, I fink I 'ave an idea wot means you won't 'ave to see the knight."

The royal children looked at Hendric and shook their heads. Tobias looked at the old man.

"What do you think you can do to help?"

"Well, I is a good shot wiv me bow, so I could shoot over the wall and let 'em know you're 'ere."

Tobias stood up and stopped Rebekah just before she got to the corner.

"Stop, Hendric has had a good idea, he can help us!"

38

The others gathered round to listen to the plan. "Princess, will you allow me to try this idea before you try yours?"

"Certainly, I would prefer not to risk being run through by a sword!"

"Good, Hendric thinks he can shoot an arrow into the castle from here letting your father know that we are here. Then maybe he can lower a rope down for us."

The others agreed that it was worth trying. Robert was fidgeting.

"What is it Robert?"

"Well, how will they know that is us and not one of the Baron's men? If they don't know it is us they might shoot arrows at us!"

"Ahhh, good point, anyone got any suggestions?"

Timothy put up his hand, then realizing he wasn't at school put it down again before anyone noticed.

"Why don't we tie a note to the arrow telling them it's us and not to shoot?"

Tobias thought about it.

"Good idea. Has anyone got something we could write on or something to write with?"

No one had.

"Any other ideas?"

Michael thought for a second then put his hand in his pocket and took a small pen-shaped object out.

"Would this tie to an arrow?"

Tobias looked at what the boy had given him and showed Hendric.

"Well, I reckon it ain't too 'eavy but 'ow we gonna fix it to the arrow?"

Adam and Nathaniel were trying to see what Michael had got from his pocket.

"What is it?" Adam asked, fed up with trying to see.

Michael took it from the old poacher and flicked a tiny switch on its side. A bright red light came out the end. Michael turned it towards the castle wall and a small red dot could be seen.

"It's dad's old laser pen from when he went to work. He gave it to me ages ago, it's one of my favorite things."

Nathaniel looked at it.

"But how will my father know it came from us?"

Tobias took it and switched it off.

"Do you know anyone else who would have something like this from the future?"

The young prince shook his head.

Rebekah had been fiddling with the hem of her dress and after her muttering there was a snap and she stood up with a length of thread and handed it to Tobias.

"Here use this."

The old man gave the boy an arrow. Everyone gathered round. Tobias carefully tied the laser pen to the arrow and handed it to Hendric He looked at it, trying to work out what it was, but he soon gave up. The old man lifted his bow and aimed it carefully. He lowered it, adjusted the string, and then raised it again. There was a slight twang and the arrow sailed up and over the wall. At the foot of the castle Nathaniel and Adam were dancing round and round.

****

In the castle the cook was not in a good mood. Not only had the kitchens been destroyed by Blackheart's trebuchet, but the King expected him to feed all of the peasants from the whole village! He and some of the castle servants had lit a fire in the courtyard. He now had a pig being turned on a spit by one of the village urchins. Bubbling steadily at the other end of the fire, two servants had a large cauldron full of whatever vegetables they could find. As the cook went to check the pig an arrow whizzed past his head and stuck in the carcass spitting hot fat all over him. He grabbed the arrow out of the dinner and was about to throw it in the fire when something caught his attention. There was something tied to the arrow. He looked at it unsure what he was seeing.

"Guard! Come here!"

A guard came running. The cook handed him the thing.

"What do you think it is?"

"I do not know, but I think the King should see it."

And with that the guard was gone.

****

Christian and Gwendolyn were in the castle keep watching the Baron's army building up on the horizon; both could see that there was no hope. The King took his wife's hand, no words were spoken. They both knew that they would be dead by the end of the battle. Then suddenly the door was thrown open and a guard came charging in, forgetting to knock on the door and forgetting to bow.

"What is the meaning of this?" demanded the King.

"Sorry, sire but I think you should see this. The cook is preparing food for everybody and an arrow stuck into the pig that's cooking."

"There are arrows falling all around, the Baron seems to like taunting us."

"Sire this one is different, look." He handed the King the arrow with the laser pen still attached. The King looked at it and accidentally turned it on and the light shone onto the wall.

"Duncan! Come here man!"

Duncan came running and fell at his master's feet. (The old servant still hadn't got used to not having to grovel.)

"Yes master, what can I do for you?"

"Get to your feet man and look at this."

The King handed him the arrow.

"What do you think it could be?"

"Sire I don't know. I have never seen anything like it before. I wonder if it could be a sign from the children."

The Queen whirled round at the mention of the children.

"Guards! Come quickly!"

Dozens of guards rushed into the room, all with their swords drawn. One of them threw Duncan to the ground and nearly killed him as he thought that the servant had threatened the royal lady. The King stepped in between them.

"Leave him, he has done no harm, but fetch the cook at once."

Two guards ran from the room returning shortly after with the cook. A guard looked at Duncan groveling on the floor in disgust.

"Do you want me to kill him sire? Nothing would give me greater pleasure than killing one of the Baron's scum."

"Leave him!" the King demanded. He turned to the cook. "Where do you think this arrow came from?"

The cook stood and tried to gather his thoughts. Then he was allowed to sit and he looked from the King to the Queen and back again.

"Well, I was trying to prepare a meal as ordered, and I was about to see how the pig was cooking when this arrow stuck in right beside my head. It was a good thing I wasn't killed or you would have all gone hungry."

"Where did the arrow come from?" the King asked again.

"Well sire, I think it came from behind the castle, all the other arrows come from the front."

The King turned to his guard.

"Gather as many knights as you can to look along the back of the castle walls."

The guard left, upset that he had not been able to kill anyone.

After a few short minutes Duncan came running and as usual fell at the King's feet.

"Sire, I think we have found them. There is a group of children at the foot of the wall and one of them looks like the princess, but we can't be sure as it is dark."

The Queen ran from the room, followed by the King.

39

Rebekah and the boys were getting cold. Hendric had suggested making a fire but Michael had pointed out that Blackheart's men would see the flames. Tobias was looking at his watch, discreetly; he didn't want to have to explain to the old man what it was. He had tried to tell him what the laser pen was but had given up. Timothy had told him that it was magic and the old poacher had been happy with that. Tobias called Robert over.

"Look, it is going to be light soon. There is no point you and your brothers being here. You heard the Baron say he would attack at first light, I promised your father I would keep you all safe. You must go back to your time and look after your brothers and your father."

Robert looked at his new friend.

"You and my dad have had many adventures, he would not want me to leave you to be killed. We all get out of this alive or we will all die together."

Tobias put his hands on Robert's shoulders.

"Thank you."

"Shhh!" Rebekah put her finger to her mouth. "Look." She pointed up to the castle battlements. High above them the children could see people looking at them from the castle walls. As it was still dark no one was sure who they were looking at.

"Mother!"

Adam was sure it was her.

"Adam! Is that you?"

"Yes."

The Baron's knight who had been guarding the drain round the corner had heard all the commotion and came running towards the noise. Sadly for him amour makes a noise when you run in it and Hendric was waiting. The knight fell with an arrow through his head.

"Duncan, run and get a rope."

The servant ran to do the Queen's bidding. A rope was quickly found and made secure to the battlements. The end was lowered down to the children. Tobias looked at Rebekah.

"You go first Princess then your brothers. Rebekah nodded and started to climb. The Queen had forgotten her royal dignity and was almost jumping with joy as her eldest child pulled herself over the battlements. Rebekah's feet had hardly touched the ground before her mother embraced her.

The girl hugged her mother and looked across to her father.

"Father, you must call all the knights to the Great Hall at once."

The King looked at his daughter, and then turned to one of his guards.

"See to it."

The guard hit his chest with his fist and was gone. One by one the other children came tumbling over the wall onto the castle battlements. Tobias was the last one. A knight went to pull the rope up.

"Wait!"

The princess went to the wall and looked down. There below her she could see Hendric about to wade back into the moat.

"Climb up!" she ordered.

The old man looked up at the princess. He knew that as he was a poacher he was a marked man by the castle guard.

"You have my word, no one will harm you, you are under my protection."

The old man looked at the princess, nodded and started to climb. As he came over the top one of the King's guards recognized him and drew his sword. The princess stopped him.

"Did you not hear what I said? He will not be harmed, he is under my protection, him and his family. Take him to the Great Hall, and give him some food."

"But Princess…"

"DO IT NOW!"

"At once Your Highness."

The guard backed away and bowed low. Hendric also bowed as he was led away. The King looked at his wife who only looked at her daughter and smiled. She would make a great Queen someday.

No one had noticed that Adam had a bag on his back from the 21st century.

****

Word had gone round that the children were back and the Great Hall was packed. The King and his family entered from behind the throne along with the visitors. The King held up his hand and the room fell silent.

"Friends, I swore that I would see Michael returned to his brothers, and because of the dedication of a dragon, they have now been reunited."

A cheer went up. The King raised his hand again.

"The children have told me that Blackheart intends to attack this very morning, we have little time. Gather what you can and when he attacks we will be waiting for him. Some of us will pay with our lives, but I promise you that I shall fight alongside you to the bitter end. Maybe, with God's grace we shall prevail. It is only a shame that the crown was not found."

Adam walked round from behind his father, taking off the rucksack as he did so. He bowed low to his father and held out the bag.

"Son?"

"Father, please open the bag."

"Son, I am busy I don't have time for your games at the moment."

"It is not a game, please open the bag."

Christian looked at his son, Adam was always playing some game to make everyone laugh, this time he noticed that his youngest child was not trying to hide a giggle.

"OK son"

The King took what his son held out, opened it and looked inside. Slowly, hardly believing what he was seeing, he took out the box with. Without drawing a breath he opened it, took out the remains of the tattered linen bag and opened that. With shaking hands he took out the crown and gently placed it on his head. There was a mighty cheer, so loud that the windows shook.

****

Blackheart had woken feeling as if he had hit his head badly in his sleep. He had no idea how long he had been in the chair. His head felt like it was going to explode. He had had the oddest dream too. He had dreamt that the princess had tried to kill him. Maybe the ale he'd drunk had been bad.

Lord Hampstead had managed to wake him an hour before sunrise, but it had taken a lot of shaking and shouting. Now the Baron was sitting on his horse in front of his massed army in front of Orford Castle. He was glad he felt so awful, now he would show no mercy. The King and his family would suffer much more than he was suffering.

"Sir," said Lord Hampstead, mounted at his master's side.

"What?"

"It looks as though the King has withdrawn his army."

As the sun started to come up Orford Castle seemed to be quiet. A few knights walked along the battlements. Flags flew as normal, nothing looked as though the castle was at war. No one could see that inside the Great Hall all the King's men stood ready to die for their King. And their King who was wearing his crown.

Blackheart snorted.

"The old fool."

The Baron looked over his shoulder. Behind him stood an army of over 5,000. He guessed the castle, even if packed full of soldiers, which was impossible, could hold no more than half that number. He looked at Hampstead.

"This may all be over sooner than we think."

****

The cheering in the Great Hall had stopped. The King stood with his family beside him. As the sun came up it shone through the window and lit up the crown. The amber jewels shone like fire. Nathaniel stepped up to his father.

"Father, this crown was found at great cost. The cost of blood."

The King looked round, all the children were there.

"Zio gave his life freely for us so that we could bring your crown home and return the kingdom to you, our rightful King."

The boy turned, trying to hide his sadness at the loss of Zio.

The King noticed it and stopped his eldest son.

"What do you mean?" he asked, his hand on the young prince's shoulder.

The boy looked at his father. He noticed that he was looking into a caring face. Before the crown had been lost the King had had little time for his children. But the King had now realized how much they meant to him and it had become different.

"Father," the boy said tearfully, "the other boys' father, Jack, Rebekah and Adam were killed by a descendant of

Blackheart. A light came out of the sky and a lady stood there. Zio spoke to her and offered himself to bring them back to life. He died to bring your family back."

The room was silent; everyone just listened to the prince's tale. Nathaniel could take no more and he threw himself into his father's arms. The King looked down at his son.

"What the dragon did makes him a hero. From now on this day, September the 4th, will be known as 'Zio's day'."

The King called for mead and as soon as he had a goblet he lifted it and shouted, "ZIO, THE HERO!"

Another cheer went up from all in the Great Hall. Tobias and Nathaniel both felt a lump rise in their throats.

No one noticed that the small boy who had been helping the cook turn the pig when the arrow with the laser pen had just missed his head slip quietly from the room. He wanted to go and fetch something that he had hidden in the castle grounds.

40

"Sire, it is time." A knight stood at the King's side. The King nodded and looking at the people before him he felt that anything was possible for those who believe.

"Come, let us go and meet the man who wants to be King of England. Rebekah, you and your brothers will ride with me. Duncan you will take the other children to safety."

Michael looked at Duncan who had been standing at the side of the room. The boy walked over to him.

"Do you know where the arrow went that was shot into the castle by Hendric?"

"Yes, why?"

"I need the thing that was tied to it."

"Come with me."

Duncan and Michael went up to the royal rooms in the keep and found the arrow. Michael grabbed it and untied the laser pen.

"What is it young master?" Duncan inquired.

"You'll see, come on."

Michael set off running to join his brothers. Duncan did his best to keep up.

****

Tobias, Robert and Timothy stood on the battlements overlooking the battlefield. Below them they could see the Baron riding towards them with his huge army behind him. The drawbridge was lowered and the royal party rode out flanked by twenty knights either side of them. Christian had the crown on his lap covered by a cloth.

Blackheart was surprised, he had expected the King to have fled by now. He could not believe his eyes. The royal children were with him! He made a slight move of his hand and the cart containing Duncan's children was brought to him. The Baron rode on to meet the King with Lord Hampstead at his side. They met halfway between the castle and the Baron's army. Blackheart was the first to speak.

"So, you have come to beg for your life and the life of your children! You forget I have sworn to destroy you all."

The King looked the evil man in the eyes and spoke very calmly.

"I have not come to beg, I will not grovel to a swine like you. We have come to accept your surrender."

The Baron laughed so much that he nearly fell of his horse. He made another slight move and his army drew closer. The cart was brought over to the Baron and he removed the cover from it. On the battlements Duncan saw his children for the first time in years.

"Ruth, David!" the old man's voice could be heard to cry out across the battlefield.

"I see that my former slave has recognized his children," the Baron sneered. "He will now see them die!"

The cart also contained wood in it and the logs were taken by two of the Baron's men and put in a heap. The bound children were roughly grabbed and thrown on top. Fire was brought from the camp.

The King stood in his saddle.

"You will not hurt the children while I am King of England!"

Blackheart pointed at Christian.

"But you are no longer the King, you are a pathetic former king. You have no crown and you call yourself a king."

The King looked Blackheart in the eye.

"Don't be so sure".

He lifted the cloth from in front of him and took out his crown. He held it aloft so that all could see and the crown shone in the morning light. He put it on his head and a mighty cheer went up from all along the castle battlements. Then the King's army started to stream out of the castle entrance. Behind the Baron some of his army fell to their knees, no longer willing to fight the rightful King of England. Blackheart was paralyzed. How could this be! He had never expected that the crown would be found. He tried to talk but could not find the words.

"You will not harm the children!"

The Baron regained himself and lunged for the king.

"Now you will die!"

Michael switched on the laser pen and shone it towards the Baron. The light played across Blackheart's helmet and reflected into his face. Blackheart was confused for a second as he tried to work out where the light came from. Enough time for the King's guards to knock the sword from his hand and to take him prisoner.

Lord Hampstead fell on his knees.

"Have mercy sire, have mercy!"

Two of the King's men had ridden over to Duncan's children and grabbed them as the fire was lit. The two of the Baron's men who had tried to kill them ran as fast as they could to get to the safety of the Baron's army; they did not make it. The King's men caught them easily and killed them.

The King's men were still streaming out of the castle, across the drawbridge and charging towards the Baron's army. The King stood in his saddle (without falling out). His army stopped just short of the archers' range. King Christian looked at the pathetic lord at his feet.

"Get up. You will come with me."

One of the twenty royal guards pulled Lord Hampstead and dragged him to his feet, while another one pulled Blackheart off his horse, a dagger at his throat. Both men were bound by the hands and then tied behind a horse. Christian turned to his Queen.

"Take our children and these prisoners back to the safety of the castle. Duncan's children are to be fed and cleaned and handed back to their father."

The Queen looked at her husband and smiled.

"At once my lord."

She turned her horse and with the others rode back to her home. Blackheart and Hampstead ran behind the horses, humiliated and alone with their thoughts.

The King and the rest of his personal guards rode towards Blackheart's army. The army was stunned and watched and waited to see what the King would do. The Earl of Bristol's soldiers were the first the King approached. Their new leader, a young knight called Sir Newton, turned to his knights.

"Take a knee! Or face my sword!" he ordered.

His knights looked at each other then one by one bowed before their King.

The King rode along the line of the Baron's men. Some bowed and some did not. The King addressed them, the sun catching the amber in his crown and making it look like fire.

"Soldiers of Blackheart, you have seen that your leader has been taken without bloodshed. It is my wish that none of you will perish needlessly today, the choice is yours. You all have the right to step behind my knights and join with me, the true King of England, and help to free this land from evil men so that all people can live in freedom and safety. If you choose to follow me I will show you mercy. If you acknowledge me as King of England I will blot out your loyalty to Blackheart and I will return you to your families unhurt. Or you can choose to take up arms against me and be destroyed. As you can see most of your comrades have bowed to me, join them or die!"

Sir Newton looked at his men and without a word to them he remounted his horse and rode behind the King's lines. His knights looked at each other and followed their leader.

"Welcome, Sir Newton Earl of Bristol. Are there any more of you?"

A few knights and their men joined the King, some did not. A small group of knights charged the King and his guards from the far end of the Baron's army. Sir Newton turned to his men.

"We will defend the King's honor, come men follow me!"

The Baron's men were destroyed before they even got close to the King.

Some of the Baron's men began to see the power of the true King and they were afraid to attack him and be slaughtered. Slowly households began to break up, most joining the King and his men. A few of the Baron's men held out hoping that somehow their lord would be able to win through.

Christian looked to his men.

"You will stay here to ensure that none of the Baron's men attack the castle. If they try you are to leave none of them standing, is that clear? Bring the leader of each household who fight under Blackheart's banner to the Great Hall."

The King's personal bodyguard moved to obey. Some of the Baron's men came willingly some were dragged, but they all came, leaving their men leaderless on the battlefield.

41

Baron Blackheart and Lord Hampstead were thrown to the floor in front of the throne in the Great Hall. The Queen looked at them. She wanted to order their deaths herself but she knew that that her husband had plans for them. Instead she ordered a guard to stand behind each of them with a sword at their necks.

"If either of them moves so much as an inch you are to show no mercy, you will kill them, is that clear?"

"Yes my lady," they replied.

The Baron felt the cold steel of the sword at his neck and he shivered. He had killed or ordered the killing of many people before but this was the first time he had felt the point of a sword and for the first time he felt fear. Hampstead was used to the feel of fear; after all he worked for the Baron.

Duncan's children had been sent to the kitchen and fed. They had both eaten as though it was the first food that they had seen in days, which it had been. A soldier was dispatched to the battlements to get Duncan.

"Sir, my Queen asks that you and the children join her in the Great Hall now."

Duncan looked at the children and Rebekah took charge.

"If my mother wants us in the Great Hall then we must go, come on."

Adam was going to complain as he wanted to stay and

watch his father's army destroy the Baron's men, but he thought better of it and followed his sister.

The Baron was still on his knees when the children entered the room. Michael was the first to see the man who had wanted him dead. He said nothing to anyone but he walked over to the cowering man. The boy looked at one of the soldiers guarding the men and held out his hand.

"Give me a sword."

The knight looked round to see what he should do, but there was no one to help him. Michael looked into the face of the guard,

"I said give me the sword". Michael spoke softly but everyone who heard knew it was not a question but a command. The guard looked at the boy in front of him and slowly handed him the sword. Blackheart let out a small sigh as the sword was removed from his neck. He wondered if he were to make a run for it how far he would get? He did not have time. Michael stood in front of the cowering former Master of Framlingham and felt the weight of the sword in his hand. The man could feel his heart beating fast in his chest. The boy allowed the man to see the sword. Everyone in the room was silent, no one even moved. Tobias wanted to call out to his friend but no words came. Michael knelt in front of the man kneeling before him. He took the Barons face in his small hand. The sweat ran down the Barons face and through the boys fingers. Blackheart could feel the boys eyes stare deep into his black soul.

"You tried to have me killed. You hate me and my brothers

and you want us all dead, don't you?"

The Baron said nothing but he knew that the boy's words were true.

Michael put the sword in front of the man's face.

"Now it is in my power to kill you, I have the sword and you are groveling on the floor, the way you made me grovel. How does it feel to know that you are about to die?"

Still the Baron said nothing, he just waited for the sharp pain as the sword entered his body. He wondered how long it would take to die.

"I am not like you. You will remember this day for the rest of your miserable life. I have a father who has always taught me right from wrong. I am not going to harm you although you deserve it."

He threw the sword on the floor behind him, and as it landed with a clang one of the King's guards picked it up. Michael again took hold of the Barons face and said nothing he just let the Baron squirm. Blackheart wanted to die now more than he had ever done before. He knew he would never forget the boy's face as long as he lived. Death would be easier than the memory. Michael stood up and appeared to tower over the man at his feet.

"I have more power than you will ever have because I forgive you. I forgive you for trying to kill me. I forgive you for wanting to destroy my family and this country. You are nothing, you thought you were the most powerful person in the land but the truth is you are just a small minded man. People like you will never come to anything, to be truly great you have to put others before yourself. My father always told me that evil will never win, and he is right. You will never rule this land because you want to kill anyone who disagrees with you. You are forgiven but remember this, if you don't change you will only destroy yourself."

Michael turned his back on the man and walked back to his brothers, never once looking back. Blackheart fell to the floor a broken man. He had been defeated by a small boy who looked right into his soul and told him what he already knew. The Great Hall was silent no one moved or spoke, never had anyone heard anyone speak like that.

The King had entered the room while Michael had been talking and had stood stunned at the young man's words. Christian strode forward to the throne and stood in front of the prisoners. Hampstead was still on his knees, head bowed to the ground. Blackheart lay at the King's feet.

"Stand before your King!"

Both men were roughly grabbed and pulled to their feet. Christian looked from one to the other.

"If it was not for this young man I would have had you killed as an example to your men. However, if the child you tried to kill can show mercy then I can do no less. You will be stripped of your lands and titles and will never be able to raise an army again!"

The men said nothing, they both knew that they had been defeated.

"Duncan, approach the throne!"

The old servant came slowly forward his head bowed.

"Hold your head up man! Look at these men before you.

Blackheart stole your lands and family, he treated you as a slave and threatened to kill your children. This day by royal decree your lands and family will be returned to you."

The King looked at one of his guards and nodded. The guard opened the door beside him and Duncan's children ran into the room.

"Father!"

Both David and Ruth threw themselves into their father's arms. Duncan said nothing; the tears running down his cheeks said it all.

Christian beckoned to his wife, and she walked to join her husband. Her children, Tobias and the others from the future joined the King and Queen at the front of the Great Hall beside the throne. Blackheart and Hampstead were forced back to their knees in front of the royal family. Duncan turned to leave holding his son by one hand and his daughter by the other.

"Duncan, where do you think you are going?"

"Sorry sire, I thought that I would return to my castle."

"Kneel before me."

Duncan, confused, knelt at Christian's feet. He thought he was no longer a servant but now he had to kneel again. The old man looked at his master. Christian looked at one of his knights and nodded. The knight stepped smartly forward and drew his sword. He handed it to the King who approached the kneeling servant. He touched the old man on the shoulder with the blade then lightly touched him on the other.

"Arise Lord Woodbridge, Lord and Master of

Framlingham and Woodbridge."

Lord Woodbridge stood and although he spoke no one heard because of the cheering. The King held up his hand and all was quiet again.

"You and your family will be protected by royal command for five generations. You will be my personal adviser and will be well paid for your work. Your first duty to your King is to take your children home and relearn how to be a father to them. Your second duty is to take these traitors before you and imprison them in your dungeon for the rest of their lives."

Duncan hugged his children.

"Yes sire," he managed to say through the tears.

"Sir Newton, come here."

The young nobleman bowed before his King.

"You and your men will order Blackheart's men to disband and return to their lands."

"At once my lord, and can I say how grateful I am that you have shown…"

"Enough, I have not forgotten that you were a member of the former Baron's army, get on with my orders!"

The young man said nothing, he just backed out of the hall, bowing as he went, and went to do as he was told.

****

At the back of the room the door opened and the small boy crept back in carrying something in a basket. Because of all the commotion going on in the Great Hall no one noticed as he walked towards the front of the room.

****

Rebekah went and spoke quietly in her father's ear. The King looked at his daughter and nodded. Rebekah held up her hand and the room fell silent.

"Hendric! Come forward!"

The old man had been sitting at the back of the hall with a guard beside him. The guard had wanted to kick the rogue out of the Great Hall but he had remembered what the princess had told him. As the princess called for the old man the guard drew his sword and prodded him towards the throne. Rebekah was furious and at once she left her family and stormed towards them. The guard realized he had done something wrong.

"How dare you force him up to me at the point of a sword like a common criminal! Don't you know what this man has done?"

The guard struggled for words.

"But Your Highness, he is a common criminal."

The girl said nothing she just brushed the guard away and led Hendric to her father. Turning to the crowd she called for them to be still.

"It is because of the bravery of this man that we are here now. If it hadn't been for him my brothers and I along with our friends would still be outside of the castle and probably dead."

The King stepped forward and put his hand on his daughter's shoulder. The princess stepped back.

"You have heard what your princess has said, From now on this man is a freeman of this castle. Hendric, your past crimes are now pardoned. From this day forward you and your family will never need to hunt for food or make do with old clothes. The cottage that once belonged to Tregore is now yours. Guards see to it that this man is treated with respect and that he is sent from here with everything he needs to furnish his new home."

The guards scurried to do the King's bidding. Hendric was speechless as he turned from the King with a new life ahead of him for his family.

****

The small boy had now reached the front of the crowd and was trying to attract Nathaniel's attention.

42

It was Adam who saw the small boy waving at his brother. He nudged Nathaniel and pointed to the child.

"I think he wants you."

The young prince looked at his younger brother and then looked to where he was pointing.

"I think you are right." And he beckoned to the boy. "Come here then."

The small boy walked towards the prince with the basket clutched to his chest. A guard tried to stop him but Nathaniel waved him away.

"Come on lad, no one will hurt you, what have you got in your basket?"

Tobias, Robert and his brothers all tried to peer into the basket to see what the boy carried. The boy held it out to Nathaniel.

"It's for you not them."

The other children along with the King and Queen tried not to laugh.

The prince took the basket. There seemed to be something in it covered by a cloth, and it was shaking.

"What is it?"

"Well I was in here when you told everyone about your dragon wot died, so I thought you would want this."

The lad removed the cloth and under it was an egg, a very big egg. At once he was grabbed by a guard and pinned to the ground, a sword at his throat. The guard looked at the boy.

"Where did you get that? No one is allowed to take dragon eggs, as they can remain dormant for years and are royal property. This crime is punishable by instant death."

"Please sir, I didn't mean any harm."

The prince knocked the guard's sword out of the way and he looked at the man.

"When I told the child that no harm would come to him I meant it. Get out of the way. Come lad you are safe. Tell me where did you get the egg?"

"Me muvver found it when she was little, and she gave it to me."

"Where is your mother now?"

"She's dead. She gave it to me when she woz sick."

The King beckoned to Lord Woodbridge and spoke in his ear. Duncan nodded. Everyone stopped as a loud crack could be heard. Nathaniel looked at the egg. A large crack appeared along its length, followed by another one. The children crowded round the egg and watched as slowly a nose appeared. Slowly and with a lot of struggling a very small baby dragon forced its way out of the egg. Nathaniel looked at the small boy in front of him.

"Thank you. What is your name?"

"Jonathan."

"Where do you live Jonathan?"

The child shrugged his shoulders and looked at the floor.

"I don't live nowhere; I just sleep where I can."

Gwendolyn looked at the child and was about to say

something but the King stopped her. He walked over to the boy.

"Do you know who I am, child?"

"Course I do, I ain't stupid. You're the King."

Christian was taken aback by the child's honesty. He beckoned Duncan over.

"Do you know who this is?"

"No, but he's old ain't he?"

The King smiled.

"This is Lord Woodbridge, and he lives in Framlingham Castle. He is in need of a stable boy. You will be well fed and looked after and have your own bed to sleep in. Would you like that?"

"Me own bed? Cor not arf!"

"Then it's settled. Duncan, this child is now your responsibility, look after him well."

"I will sire, I will."

Duncan took the boy by the hand and led him to meet his children.

Nathaniel was holding a baby dragon in his hands surrounded by his friends. He looked at his father with tears in his eyes.

"I'm going to call him Zeo, in memory of Zio, is that all right?"

"Yes son, it is fine."

The King held up his hand and all the chatter in the Great Hall died away. He called all the royal children to him, and beckoned to Tobias, Robert and his brothers.

"Friends, these children came from the future to help save

this kingdom, and they have now done so. It is time for them to return to their own time and their father. Robert, you said that you came through what is now Hendric's cottage, is that correct?"

"Yes Your Highness."

"Good, we will escort you all home. Guards! Arrange a guard of honor for these children. Duncan, you and I along with my children will accompany them to the cottage. Gwendolyn, you will stay here with Duncan's children and the young stable boy. You are to make sure the boy is washed and given some clean clothes."

The Queen nodded and said nothing. Since the boys from the future had arrived in her castle she had seen her husband become the King that the country needed.

****

The cottage was still and in darkness. Robert, Michael and Timothy were excited about going home. Hendric was excited about seeing his new home. The King turned to Robert.

"May I come into the cottage with you or do you want to go in just with your brothers?"

Michael spoke up for Robert.

"Please could we just go in with your children and Tobias?"

"Of course you may."

The King and his knights stood away from the door. The seven children went into the cottage. It was just as they remembered it. Tobias shut the door behind him.

Suddenly the room was filled with light and Obney stood in the middle of the room. A great peace entered the room.

The King and his men outside were dazzled by the light. Hendric wanted to go in but the King stopped him.

"Go and get your family and bring them to your new home."

The old man looked at the King and bowed, then he hurried off to find his wife and daughter.

Obney looked at the children and addressed Tobias.

"Tobias you have fulfilled your mission and helped to return this land to peace. You will soon go home but I will allow you to say goodbye to your new friends. Robert, Timothy and Michael you have done better than I could have hoped. You will go forward and do more missions with Tobias, will you accept this calling?"

Timothy felt his heart beat a bit faster as he nodded.

"Come forward."

Obney held out her hand and gave each of the brothers a small watch that they put on.

"Whenever I need your help these watches will flash and you will have two minutes before you will be called to your next mission. Princess Rebekah, you and your brothers must return to your father's castle where in time you will help to rule this country. I will call on you also from time to time when I need you."

She held out her hand and gave the royal children each an amulet.

"The time has come."

Turning to the fireplace Obney moved her hand and the door opened.

The children hugged each other. All with tears in their eyes.

Tobias said what they were all thinking.

"This isn't really goodbye, more like see you soon."

Robert looked at the princess then he walked over to her and tried to speak but could not find the words. He looked at his feet and fidgeted a bit. Then he looked at her and took hold of her and kissed her on the cheek before going back to his brothers. Rebekah went red and for the first time in ages she could think of nothing to say. Timothy looked back at his friends one last time before stepping into the passage followed by his brothers. The door closed behind them. Tobias and Obney were left alone with the royal children. The door slowly disappeared from view and where it once had been there was only the wall, you would never have guessed there had ever been a door there. Obney looked at the children and smiled, she looked at Tobias and nodded. He went and stood with her. There was a blinding flash and the princess found herself alone in the room with her brothers. She took hold of her brothers' hands and led them out of the cottage and into the woods. She went up to her father.

"They have gone home, Tobias as well. We at last have peace in this land."

The King nodded and led the party back to the castle.

****

Timothy and his brothers ran through the tunnel to their home. Timothy was the first to reach the door. He threw the door open and rushed up the stairs into the hall.

"Dad! What's for tea I'm hungry?"

ZIO THE HERO

ABOUT THE AUTHOR

Marc Grimston has always been a story teller, writing poetry and short stories throughout his adult life. When challenged to write a children's novel, Marc reluctantly agreed. Although comfortable making-up stories for his children at bed time, creating an adventure for them to read for themselves, seemed a big step.

Marc believes in the value of self-worth. With dedication and determination, you can achieve anything. Through his writing, Marc wants to empower and encourage all children to reach and achieve their goals.

Marc is in contact with several UK schools to work with them to encourage literacy, story-telling and the belief that all things are possible.

Marc takes walks along the beach, when not writing more thrilling adventures in his home town of Southend-on-Sea in Essex.

Printed in Great Britain
by Amazon.co.uk, Ltd.,
Marston Gate.